MIDDLE SCHOOL
MY BROTHER IS A BIG, FAT LIAR

JAMES PATTERSON is one of the best-known and biggest-selling writers of all time. He is the internationally bestselling author of the highly praised Middle School books, *Treasure Hunters*, and the I Funny, Confessions, Maximum Ride, Witch & Wizard and Daniel X series. In 2010, James Patterson was voted Author of the Year at the Children's Choice Book Awards in New York. He lives in Florida.

MIDDLE SCHOOL

MY BROTHER IS A BIG, FAT LIAR

James Patterson

AND LISA PAPADEMETRIOU

ILLUSTRATED BY NEIL SWAAB

Published by Young Arrow, 2014

2 4 6 8 10 9 7 5 3 1

Copyright © James Patterson, 2013
Illustrations by Neil Swaab

James Patterson has asserted his right under the Copyright, Designs
and Patents Act 1988 to be identified as the author of this work

First published in Great Britain in 2013 by
Young Arrow
Random House, 20 Vauxhall Bridge Road,
London SW1V 2SA

www.randomhouse.co.uk

Addresses for companies within The Random House Group Limited can be found at:
www.randomhouse.co.uk/offices.htm

The Random House Group Limited Reg. No. 954009

A CIP catalogue record for this book is available from the British Library

ISBN 9780099567875

The Random House Group Limited supports the Forest Stewardship
Council® (FSC®), the leading international forest-certification organisation.
Our books carrying the FSC label are printed on FSC®-certified paper. FSC is the only
forest-certification scheme supported by the leading environmental organisations,
including Greenpeace. Our paper procurement policy can be found at:
www.randomhouse.co.uk/environment

Printed and bound in Great Britain by Clays Ltd, St Ives Plc

For Marguerite Belkin

—L.P.

CHAPTER 1

Rafe Is a Big, Fat Liar

It isn't easy having a brother who's famous in all the wrong ways. It also isn't easy having a brother who's a blabbermouth. I'm sure Rafe has told you all about me. Let's see—what did he say? That I'm a tattletale? That I get on his nerves? That I always eat all the pudding cups?

Well, I have news for you: Lies. All lies.

WANTED

FOR UNSPEAKABLE MISCHIEF IN MIDDLE SCHOOL — DISRESPECT FOR RULES AND REGULATIONS, PUTTING GRAFFITI IN PUBLIC PLACES, TRUANCY, BODY ODOR, UNFUNNY BATHROOM HUMOR, SIBLING TORTURE

I did it, and I'm **GLAD!**

Except the pudding-cup thing. That's…well, okay, that's accurate.

Let me make one thing perfectly clear: Rafe Khatchadorian is a big, fat liar. And just to prove I'm the kind of girl who tells the truth, I will now correct myself: Rafe is actually a skinny, normal-size liar. And his version of me is completely out of whack.

Here's the *real* story: Rafe does crazy stuff all the time, and nobody ever gets on his case about it. He just gets yanked out of sixth grade and sent to art school.

But when *I* do something wrong?

So what is Georgia Khatchadorian really like?
Well, I'm much smarter than Rafe. Just ask the
people who write the State Intelligence Assessment
Tests.

Also, I'm hilarious.

MY FAVORITE RAFE JOKE

Actually, I'm usually pretty kind. (Rafe thinks *I* tattletale? You should hear the stuff I *haven't* told!)

I have excellent fashion sense, which I choose not to express. This is because I'm always broke.

And I'm the innocent victim of my brother's slander.

So I guess this story is about what happens when a smart, kind, creative girl tries to live down her brother's bad reputation.

It's really not my fault that it all blew up in my face.

CHAPTER 2

Don't Mess with a Khatchadorian

Fifty-five minutes until my first day at Hills Village Middle School, and I was stuck at the breakfast table with Captain Irritation.

"What is that? Rabbit poop?" Rafe asked, eyeing my cereal.

"It's muesli," I said.

"Moose pee?"

My older brother is sooooo sophisticated. "Muesli is like granola," I told him. "They eat it in Europe."

"They also eat slugs in Europe," Rafe pointed out.

"Snails," I corrected. "Escargot."

Rafe rolled his eyes. "That word even *sounds* like barf."

I looked over at Mom. Her face was quivering, as if she couldn't decide whether to laugh or frown. I love my mom, and I have no idea how she can find Rafe funny. It must be a gene I missed.

"So, are you two excited for your first day?" Mom asked.

Changing the subject. Nicely done, Mom.

"I can't wait," Rafe and I said together. Only his voice clearly meant "I *can* wait," while my voice meant "I'm so excited that I'm about to explode!"

Rafe snorted. "You're nuts."

"Just because you didn't like sixth grade doesn't mean that I won't."

"Yeah, because you're nuts." He narrowed his eyes at me. "It's like prison in there. You'll get eaten alive, Little Miss Pink Backpack with a Pony on It," he growled.

"Mom!" I screeched.

"That's enough, Rafe," Mom said, casting a worried glance my way. "Stop trying to scare Georgia." I knew she was nervous about my first day. After all, Rafe had had a pretty rough sixth-grade year.

RAFE'S SIXTH-GRADE YEAR

What? Did you just say I shouldn't worry, because *my brother is a big, fat liar*?

Hey—watch it. I can talk all I want about my brother, but nobody else can say bad things about him. I have Rafe's back. Mostly to throw stuff at, and for the occasional backstabbing.

The point is—his back is *mine*, not yours.

And even though my brother *is* a big, fat liar, I had a bad feeling he was telling the truth this time.

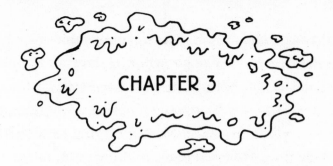

CHAPTER 3

Horrors of an (In)Famous Brother

The good news is that nobody cared about my backpack. The bad news is that Rafe was right—HVMS *is* like prison. My crime? Mistaken identity.

It wasn't bad at first. I didn't really mind that the school bus smelled like an armpit. I didn't even mind that all the kids seemed to know one another already.

Then I got to homeroom. I'd never had to change classes before, so I was nervously trying to memorize my schedule while the teacher, Mr. Grank, called roll. He suddenly said, "Georgia Khatchadorian? You're Rafe Khatchadorian's SISTER?!" Yup, he said it just like that, in all-capital letters, with an exclamation point at the end.

I thought the Khatchadorian species was EXTINCT!

Not extinct. we've just evolved.

The class went silent. Then everyone started whispering to one another.

I felt myself blush. "Um...yeah?" I said, hesitating.

"You don't *know*?" Mr. Grank growled.

"Well, sir...I was just hoping, maybe we could keep that, um, little piece of trivia just between me, you, and these four walls?"

I grinned nervously, but Mr. Grank was all "Don't get smart with me, Ms. Khatchadorian."

Someone in the class said, "Ooooh, *trivia*..." and I felt everyone looking at me, like I was showing off some big, fancy vocabulary word or something. Actually, it was more like they thought I was going to take off all my clothes and streak through the hallway. (Which Rafe actually did once.) So I slumped down in my chair until the bell rang.

Now, normally we would've gone to a Big School Assembly next to learn about the school rules and stuff. But for some reason—(ahem, *Rafe*)—there wasn't one this year. The Code of Conduct was being "reworked." So we went straight to our classes.

Anyone want to guess why—(cough, cough, *Rafe*)—the teacher gave me a "special welcome" in English? And math? And French? And gym?

For those of you who are confused right now because you don't know much about Rafe, here's the deal: He's notorious around here because he tried to break every single rule in the student handbook. He almost did it too, but he got kicked out. (If you're interested in knowing even more about it, just read *Middle School, The Worst Years of My Life*. Personally, I wouldn't bother. But you might like it... if you're crazy.)

17

And now everybody at HVMS seemed to think I was going to be the next crazy Khatchadorian.

Everywhere I went, I was following in my brother's muddy, bloody footsteps. I was about as popular as toxic waste. Rafe wasn't even here, and he'd already ruined everything.

But I'm not Rafe. I'm the kind of girl who gets straight A's. I even won Most Outstanding Effort in the third grade. All these people have the wrong idea about me.

I decided that I'd just have to show them that I'm not Rafe Khatchadorian II: The Revenge. I'm more like Georgia Khatchadorian I: The Relatively Normal.

I thought that once I showed everyone the real me, things would get better.

Boy, was I wrong.

CHAPTER 4

Miller the (Mini) Killer

And then there was lunch. Students everywhere, and not a friend in sight.

Oh, but there was a *fiend* in sight. It seems that my brother's old buddy, Miller the Killer, has a little brother. And by *little*, I mean *enormous*. I'd seen Miller—and Mini-Miller looks just like him. Only bigger and uglier.

I was standing at the front of the cafeteria when he walked up to me. "Muuuuuunh," he grunted. "Muuuuuuunh." He was dragging his leg behind him.

Then he grinned a stupid grin at me.

"Are you supposed to be a zombie?" I asked. "Because clearly someone has eaten your brain."

He narrowed his piggy eyes at me. "You're Rafe Khatchadorian's sister, right?" Mini-Miller plucked my chocolate chip cookie right off my tray and ate it in a single gulp.

"What makes you say that?" I replied.

Mini-Miller glared. "It says 'Khatchadorian' on your notebook."

"Oh, you can read that?" I asked. That must have been the wrong thing to say, because he flipped my lunch tray right out of my hands. Food splattered all over the floor, and the hard plastic tray landed with a clatter that rang through the cafeteria.

"Oops," Mini-Miller said. Then he laughed, stomped on my foot, and walked away.

Maybe Rafe isn't so bad....

CHAPTER 5

Rhonda Helps Me, Helps, Helps Me, Rhonda

NEED SOME HELP?" someone asked in a screechy voice that made my eardrums want to shrivel up and die. She sounded like the Screecher from the Black Lagoon.

When I turned and saw where the voice came from, I jumped. She didn't just sound like a screechy Creature from the Black Lagoon. She, uh, kind of looked like it too. And she was dressed in what looked like a costume straight out of the 1950s.

Not to mention the girl was huge. Okay, that's

softening it. She was fat. I'm sorry, but it's true. Some people look like manatees that have escaped from a musical theater production. Some people look like supermodels. I'm not judging, just stating facts. I'm no supermodel myself. You've seen the pictures.

I'll say one other thing: In a cafeteria full of kids, the Screecher was the only one who stood up to help. So she actually looked pretty good to me.

The Screecher flipped over my tray and started piling my cup, plate, and bowl on it. "I'M RHONDA," she said, grinning up at me. She had a really friendly smile—white teeth and a dimple in her left cheek.

By Rafe Khatchadorian

"Oh. Hi." I squatted to gather my silverware.

"YOU HAVE MASHED POTATO ON YOUR SHIRT," Rhonda told me.

I sighed.

"AND YOUR FACE," she added.

I let my silverware clatter onto the plastic tray. "Do you know where the girls' room is?"

"DOWN THE HALL, TO YOUR LEFT. WANT ME TO SHOW YOU?"

"No, that's okay. I've got it." I took the tray from her hands. "Thanks."

"ANYTIME!" Another bright smile, and then she stomped back to her seat. She walked like she talked: loudly.

So, in half a day, I'd met Mini-Miller and the Screechy Creature from the Grease Lagoon. Surely HVMS couldn't produce anything weirder—right?

Wrong.

CHAPTER 6

The Princess Patrol!

When I left the cafeteria, the noise suddenly died down (and I'm not just talking about Rhonda). The only students in the hall were three girls clustered around a locker, and they all looked like they'd been dressed by the same celebrity stylist. They eyed me for a minute, and then one put up her hand to shield a whisper. The others laughed.

I'd seen them before. All three are in my French class. Missy Trillin is clearly in charge of, like, the entire school. And everyone in it. In class earlier today, a nerdy boy with glasses had made the mistake of sitting in the seat she wanted.

That's Fabio's seat.

She means my throne!

Missy's family is incredibly rich. Her mother invented Mac N Cheesyohs—you know, macaroni-and-cheese on a stick that you heat up in the toaster—so they have gobs of money. Everyone wants to dress like Missy. Everyone wants to go to her parties. Everyone wants to ride in her solid-gold limousine.

The two celebutantes with Missy were named Brittany and Bethany, but I wasn't sure which was which. Looking at them, I finally understood what Rafe had meant about my pony backpack. These girls had clothes that made my T-shirt and jeans look like sewn-together old dish towels. Their perfect skin made my face look like someone had attacked me with a permanent marker. Their white teeth could've blinded anyone within fifteen feet of them, and you could probably lose a pet Chihuahua somewhere in the middle of their thick, puffy hairstyles. (In fact, Missy actually did have a pet Chihuahua.) I felt like I'd just wandered into a shampoo commercial they were starring in.

Their eyes were on me as I walked along, looking for the girls' room. It wasn't where I expected it to be, but I kept hoping it would appear, like an oasis in the desert.

"Clip-clop," Missy said, and the B's cracked up.

I didn't know what that meant, but it was clearly a joke, so I chuckled along.

"Um, hi," I said with a smile. "Can you tell me where the girls' room is?"

Missy gave me a pursed-lips smile that twisted up the side of her mouth. "Do I *know* you?" she asked. Her voice made it clear that she couldn't *possibly* know me. She gave me an up-and-down look that made me want to go hide out in a locker for the rest of the year.

"I don't think we know anyone who gets her clothes out of a Dumpster," one of the B's said.

"Or cuts her hair with a Weedwacker," added the other.

Clearly, these girls were grade-A snobs. So I was all "I guess you guys blew off a couple of lessons at charm school, because that was seriously rude." And then they burst into tears, and Missy tried to draw me a map to the girls' room, but I just walked off.

Well, okay, not exactly true. I *did* just walk off. But I didn't think of that witty comeback until three days later.

"Clip-clop!" Missy called after me. Her little

friends laughed, and they all took off, prancing
down the hall like show ponies.

Great. Now they have some little inside joke.
Clip-clop. What did that mean?

I came up with a few possibilities:

1. Misheard "tick-tock": Missy and the B's
   planted a bomb somewhere in building; need
   to notify security PRONTO for disciplinary
   action.

2. Princess lingo picked up at expensive riding
   academy: They had a secret horse language
   only they could understand.

3. Insult to my footwear: It was, admittedly, not
   nearly as chic as theirs.

I wasn't really sure which choice was correct,
but—based on their personalities—my guess was
number three. Though I went ahead and pretended
it was number one.

Soooooo…now I had Grank and Screecher, a
Mini-Miller, *and* a Princess Patrol to deal with.
Could this day get any worse?

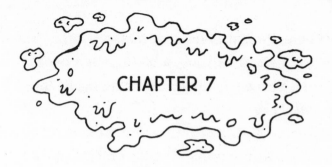

CHAPTER 7

The Awesomes!

School ended about five million hours later. By the end of the day, I felt like I should just get *I AM RAFE KHATCHADORIAN'S SISTER* tattooed across my forehead to save everyone the trouble of mentioning it.

When the last bell rang, Missy climbed into her jewel-studded limo, and I headed back to my bus. Three whiplash-inducing miles later, I was safely home with my friends Nanci, Mari, and Patti. (Yes, they let me hang out with them, even though my name doesn't end in an *i* and we don't go to the same school.) We were sitting at the kitchen table, munching warm chocolate chip cookies that my Grandma Dotty, who lives with us now, had made.

"So, Georgia!" Mari smiled through her crumbs. "Are we ready to rock?"

"Absolutely," I said.

"Just one more cookie," Nanci said, grabbing five. I have no clue why she's so thin.

"What happened to your shirt?" Patti asked.

"Mashed potatoes," I explained. "Someone flipped them on me."

"That is *so* wasteful." Patti shook her head as she smoothed her natural-fiber batik shirt. Patti is very eco-friendly.

"Next time, I'll give the guy a lecture," I promised.

Then we headed out to the garage to practice.

I turned on my amp and strummed my electric guitar. Yes, that's right, I'm in a

Ich eally ool!

Nanci, Mari, and Patti are friends I made over the summer. They all go to Rafe's school, Airbrook Arts, and I met them at the spring picnic. Mom insisted that we all go to it, since Rafe would be starting at Airbrook in the fall. We brought dessert, which is helpful for making friends with food-eating machines like Nanci.

Patti and Mari were with her. We started talking about baking, then about art (Nanci makes awesome sculptures, and Mari and Patti are into painting), and then about music. It turns out that Nanci plays drums, Mari plays bass, and Patti plays the keyboard. "All we need is an electric guitarist," Mari said.

So I said,

The next day I picked up my electric guitar and amp at a tag sale. Grandma Dotty loves tag sales, and somehow she managed to bargain with the guy who was selling them, until we paid just three dollars for both. And the rest is history.

Well...it *will be* history. Once we're famous.

Naturally, Rafe was furious that I'd actually made friends at Airbrook Arts before he did, which only made me even *happier* to be in the band. We're called the Awesomes! It's our dream to play the school dance this year.

Mom let us keep our equipment in the garage, so we were all set up. "Should we do our theme song?" I asked.

"Let's jam!" Mari shouted—and we blew the lid off that garage!

We Stink!

Um, did I say we blew the lid off the garage?

Someone knocked on the door between the kitchen and the garage. A second later, Rafe's messy-haired head was poking into my band's space.

"Get out," I said. It's a reflex.

Rafe ignored me (also a reflex). "Can I listen to you guys practice?"

"No!" I shouted, but Mari had already said, "Sure, Rafe," and Patti added, "Come on in!" So the next thing I knew, my brother was propped on a folding chair right next to the rack where we keep the extra paper towels and toilet paper. He smiled at me. I narrowed my eyes at him.

From the
Mind of
Georgia
Khatchadorian

NOTE TO SELF:
THROTTLE
RAFE LATER.

"It's really cool that you guys have started a band," Rafe said. He looked at me. "I didn't know you could play guitar."

"We wouldn't have a band without Georgia," Mari said.

"Really?" Rafe smirked in my direction. He tipped back in his chair, and I wished that it would fall over backward, dumping him onto the floor. "So, what kind of music do you play?" he asked.

"Loud," Nanci told him.

My brother grinned. "My favorite!"

Mari, Nanci, and Patti cracked up. They're really friendly, which is a pain sometimes. Like when they're being nice to my brother.

"One!" Mari called. "Two! One-two-three-four!"

We launched into our theme song again. I added a little guitar solo in the middle, but it wasn't really on purpose. My fingers just got stuck in the strings. Hey, give me a break—I've never had a single lesson, okay? I've been teaching myself by watching music videos. I can jump, twirl, even crawl on my knees while playing. I just can't really make the notes come out right.

When we finished our song, Nanci twirled a
lock of blue hair nervously. She has black hair
with turquoise streaks and likes to wear torn
jeans, combat boots, and T-shirts with cartoon
superheroes on them. "So—what did you think?"
she asked my brother.

Luckily, Rafe didn't have a chance to answer,
because just then Grandma Dotty stuck her head
through the door. "Did anyone else hear some awful

crashing and wailing just a minute ago?" she asked. "Like part of the roof caved in on a howler monkey? Or a truck full of cats tipped over?"

"Um, no," I said.

"I'd better call the ASPCA," she said, and shut the door with a slam.

"Were we that bad?" Mari asked. She was looking at Rafe, as if his opinion counted for anything.

"No." Rafe shook his head.

"Oh, good." Nanci looked relieved.

"You were way worse," Rafe added. The band looked horrified. "You guys should change your name to We Stink."

I was afraid my friends might actually walk out the garage door and never come back. "YOU stink!" I shot back. "I can smell you from over here."

"That's your breath," Rafe said.

I couldn't think of a good reply, so I grabbed a roll of toilet paper and threw it at his head. Laughing, Rafe dodged and scooted through the door.

From the Mind of. Georgia Khatchadorian

NOTE TO SELF:
THROTTLE RAFE ~~LATER~~. AS SOON AS POSSIBLE!

"Do we really stink?" Mari asked.

"Rafe would've said that no matter how good we sounded," I pointed out.

"But we *do* need more practice," Nanci admitted.

"Then let's do it!" Mari agreed.

"Rock on!" Patti cheered.

I wasn't so sure. But we launched back into our theme song, and this time it was even better than before. Now if I could just nail that guitar solo...

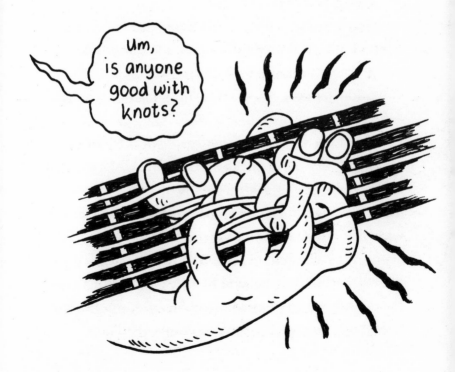

Home, Sweet Home

A pretty awesome band practice might cancel
out a pretty horrible first day of school, but when
you add them together, you still get *complete
exhaustion.*

What I need is a hug from my mom, I thought,
and to tell her all about my crazy day. Unfortunately,
Mom wasn't home, which meant no hug and no
dinner either, unless I cooked it myself. Mom is a
waitress, which means that she usually works all
evening. So we kind of have to fend for ourselves.

I wished I had someone to talk to. But Mari,
Patti, and Nanci went to Airbrook Arts, where I bet
everybody (except my brother) was cool. They

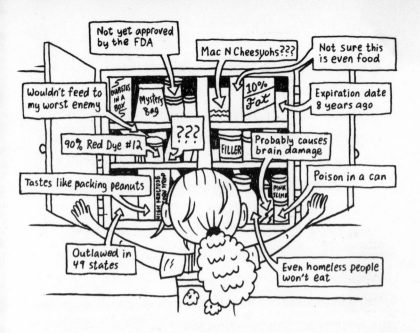

didn't know what it was like to face the snobs of the
Princess Patrol. *I could talk to Grandma Dotty*, I
thought, *but she would just tell me to be grateful that
I didn't have to walk five miles to school, the way she
used to.* And the only other person around was…

"Stinky!" Rafe announced as he strolled into the
kitchen. "That's the perfect word to describe your
band, Georgia. Seriously, I actually think We Stink
is a good name. It's kind of got a rock edge."

I just sighed. I didn't have the energy to think of
a comeback.

"What's wrong? Had a bad day?"

For a second I thought maybe he cared. Then I noticed the big grin on his face.

"My day was horrible," I snapped. "Thanks to you."

"Me?" He batted his eyelashes. "I have no idea what you're talking about." He opened the fridge, pulled out a carton of orange juice, and chugged down, like, half of it. Gross.

"You know exactly what I'm talking about," I replied. "That's some path you've blazed for me at HVMS."

"That's because I was the only interesting person who ever went there," Rafe replied. He chugged more juice.

"Yeah, I met your buddy Miller's little brother. I think we'll be hanging out a lot." My voice was dripping with sarcasm.

"Did he bother you?" Rafe asked. He didn't have a smirk on his face now.

"He's nothing I can't handle. Anyway, all my teachers are amazed that you're still in school," I told him, "instead of jail."

Rafe shrugged. "I wouldn't even call them teachers. More like wardens. Admit it—I was right and you were wrong."

^^^

List of Things I Would Rather Do Than Tell Rafe I Was Wrong

^^^

Sew an outfit for
Missy's Chihuahua.

Kiss a tarantula.

Eat brussels sprouts.

Just
tell me
you were
wrong.

I wasn't about to agree with him. "One day
doesn't mean anything," I told him, walking to the
cupboard to take out a box of pasta. "It's going to
get better."

"Wrong."

I whirled to face him. "I'm not you, Rafe. I know
how to make friends. I know how to get good
grades. I guarantee that in four weeks, I'll have
straight A's, *and* I'll be one of the most popular girls
at school."

Thanks
for putting us
onto the A+
list, Georgia!

You're
the It
Girl,
Georgia.

Cat is
the new
Dog!

Purrr...

The Princess Patrol will be begging me to hang out with them, I thought. *My teachers will have forgotten Rafe ever existed.*

"Wanna bet?" Rafe's eyebrows shot up. "In four weeks, you'll have zero friends, and you'll be begging to get out of HVMS."

I folded my arms across my chest. "Yeah. I do want to bet." The wheels were already spinning in my mind.

My brother looked a little surprised. "What should we bet?"

"Loser does the winner's chores for a month."

Rafe looked around the kitchen at the unswept floor, the dishes piled in the sink, the crumbs on the counter. The rest of our house was more of the same: like the "before" picture on a home-makeover show. There were loads of chores to be done—and I would think up plenty more when I *won*.

Rafe grinned again. "Deal," he said, and we shook on it. He seemed pretty confident.

I couldn't wait to wipe the smile right off his face...and prove to everyone that the only problem I had at HVMS was having RAFE for a brother.

Sweet Home Georgiabama

Grandma Dotty wandered into the kitchen, singing at the top of her lungs. She was wearing a tracksuit and a pair of rainbow-striped leg warmers. "I read these are making a comeback!" Grandma crowed.

Maybe in the "let's embarrass our grandkids as much as possible" universe, I thought.

I put a pot on the stove and lit the flame while Grandma Dotty belted out her rendition of "Sweet Home Alabama"...which slowly turned into a rendition of "Georgia on My Mind"...and then turned into a version of "Omaha Mall" by Justin Bieber.

Grandma's not very good with places and names. Or fashion.

Once the water started to boil, I threw in some pasta, then reached for some wilted lettuce. *Shouldn't making dinner be a grown-up's job?* I thought as Rafe chugged *more* orange juice, finishing off the carton. He let out a huge belch loud enough to rattle the dishes in the sink. Dotty giggled.

Oh, yeah, I reminded myself. *I'm the only grown-up here at the moment.*

I washed the sagging lettuce leaves and topped them with cherry tomatoes (which I love) and green pepper slices (which Rafe hates) to brighten them up and hide their age.

"First course!" I sang as I brought the plates into the dining room.

Rafe frowned at the salad. "Yeah, that's pretty appetizing—if you're a rabbit."

"I guess I was confused by your giant ears and twitchy nose," I shot back.

"This looks wonderful!" Dotty gushed. "So healthy."

Rafe picked the peppers out of his salad and

placed them on the side of his plate. He nibbled a leaf, then asked, "Where's the real food?" Like I was his servant or something.

"Next course, coming right up," I said as cheerfully as I could through gritted teeth.

Back in the kitchen, I strained the pasta and ladled on some sauce.

"Hey, Georgia, that actually doesn't look horrible," Rafe said when I placed the plate in front of him.

I smiled sweetly. "Be sure to eat it while it's nice and hot."

Rafe took a huge, greedy bite and hit the roof. Literally.

"Hot enough for you?" I asked, but Rafe didn't answer. He was too busy fanning the flames burning his lips. Hmm. I guess he didn't enjoy the entire bottle of hot sauce I emptied onto his pasta.

Good thing I didn't put any on Grandma's or mine.

Grandma took another bite. "This is delish, Carolina."

Rafe sputtered and howled. He couldn't really speak, but I knew what he was trying to say—and it involved revenge. *I'd better escape while he's busy dousing his tongue with a glass of water*, I decided. I left my dishes in the sink and headed to the one place where I knew Rafe wouldn't dare bother me.

My safe place.

CHAPTER 11

My Mom Is My Best Friend

When I got to my safe place, I discovered it had been invaded by a carnivorous (but nicely dressed) beast.

You guessed it: Missy. Sitting there in a corner booth of Swifty's Diner with her snooty-looking family. They were daintily eating apple pie.

I skulked over to the counter and slipped onto one of the red stools, holding my copy of *The Book Thief* in front of my face. *Please don't notice me*, I begged silently.

"Your mom'll be right over, Georgia honey!" Pearl hooted. Pearl is the other waitress, and she always does everything at top volume.

Cringing, I glanced at Missy. She was looking right at me with narrowed eyes and a tight little smile. I turned my back on her as the pasta in my stomach threatened to revolt. *Great. If Missy comes over, maybe I can barf on her.*

"Hi, sweetie," Mom said as she leaned across the counter and landed a kiss on my forehead.

I felt like I'd just reached a desert oasis. *Mom will know how to handle Missy*, I realized. "I need to ask you—"

"I want to hear all about it. I'll be back in a sec." She hauled a huge tray piled with dinner plates to a table by the window. It was seven o'clock, and the diner was packed.

The diner burned to the ground last year, but Swifty had rebuilt it with the help of a big insurance check, and it's way nicer now than it ever was before. And more crowded.

Swifty shouted, "Order up!" and Mom hustled over to the grill to pick up the dinners. She held up her index finger, giving me the "One minute!" signal.

Argh—I didn't have "one minute"! My problems had followed me all the way to my safe place and were threatening to *attack*.

I cast a nervous glance toward Missy's corner. Her family was getting up to leave. *Please, please, please just go*, I thought.

I hid behind my book. The librarian had tried to tell me that it would be too hard for me. She must've had me confused with Rafe. (Note to reader: Rafe has never read *The Book*

Diner camouflage

THE BOOK THIEF
MARKUS ZUSAK

Thief or any other book except the CliffsNotes for the Captain Underpants series. Okay, I'm exaggerating. He also sometimes reads the menu at McDonald's.)

A moment later, Mom brought me a glass of chocolate milk. Chocolate removed.

"How was your first day of middle school?" she asked gently, crossing her arms on the counter. Finally—some time for just Mom and me.

"Oh, it was—" I looked toward the table in the corner. Missy was gone. *Good*, I thought. *Now I can really tell Mom all about it.* "It was okay, but—"

"Excuse me?" A bald man held up his coffee cup. "Refill?"

"Sure." Mom scurried away to grab the carafe. The minute she refilled his cup, someone else was ready to order. Then another table's food was ready, people were leaving, someone dropped a spoon….Mom got caught in the chaos, and I couldn't reach her.

I wished she could just take a night off and hang out watching movies on the couch with Rafe and me. But she works too much. Even when she's around, it's hard to get her attention—because Rafe hogs it all.

I really wanted to talk to Mom about Missy...but
it looked like this wasn't my lucky night. I'd just
have to figure out what to do about the Princesses
on my own.

I would have to fight fire with fire.

The Princess Dress Code

When I came downstairs the next morning, Rafe took one look at me and nearly blew a chunk of Cap'n Crunch out his nose. He had to take a sip of juice to keep from choking on his own laughter.

"Be quiet," I told him as I slid into the chair across from his.

"You look very pretty, Virginia," Grandma Dotty said.

"Thank you."

"Something special happening at school today, honey?" Mom asked as she placed an empty bowl in front of me.

"She's trying to fit in," Rafe announced.

Okay, that's not really what I was wearing. But I couldn't believe Rafe had figured out that my oh-so-casual outfit was really oh-so-desperate. *Am I that obvious?*

"Yeah," Rafe went on, "Georgia's going to attempt to pass herself off as an earthling."

I relaxed a little. Of course Rafe didn't have me figured out. He can barely figure out how to work a toilet-paper roll.

But even though he didn't know it, he was right. I'd gotten up early and put together an outfit that looked a little bit like what Brittany and Bethany had been wearing the day before—skirt, leggings, flats, and a tunic—with a messenger bag instead of a backpack. I was going to try to blend in.

Naturally, my plan worked flawlessly. Instant popularity was mine.

"Please tell me that you got dressed in the dark this morning," Missy begged, and her friends giggled. "Nice try. I guess you're just..."—she smiled smugly—"...super lame."

"Super lame!" Brittany squealed, and she and Bethany high-fived.

Yeah, well, you're just...uh...you're a big...um—

I couldn't think of a single witty comeback. So I trudged toward my locker, trying to ignore the other kids lining the hallways.

The trick is to stay out of Missy's way, I told myself as I spun my combination lock. Most kids scattered when they saw her coming down the hall. Seriously—it was like a Godzilla movie, only scarier. I was pretty sure that one day Missy would be the first dictator of the United States.

CHAPTER 13

Not My Problem

As the Princesses strutted past my locker, I watched the other students cowering before Missy and the B's. It was like the Patrol had some kind of "loser radar"— from all the way down the hall, they could zero in on loners, nerds, and kids with less money than them. I even saw teachers duck into their classrooms to avoid the princessy sneers.

I closed the door to my locker and made my way toward class...and saw Rhonda come around the corner before Missy spotted her.

Missy was giggling at something Bethany had said, and she wasn't watching where she was going. She slammed right into Rhonda, who went down on her butt like a sack of Jell-O dressed in saddle shoes. Rhonda's armful of books scattered everywhere. Her three-ring binder opened, and papers rained down like a ticker-tape parade.

"Watch it, Chubby!" Missy snapped.

The other girls laughed.

"Yeah, are you blind?" Brittany asked. "Oh, wait—I just noticed your clothes. I guess you are!" The Princesses kept on walking.

And what did I do?

I kept on walking too. Of course.

Hey, I've got enough problems already. I've got a bet to win! Besides, I'll never make friends at this school if I go around helping people like Rhonda.

CHAPTER 14

This Is Probably a Ginormous Mistake, But...

Actually, I didn't do that.

I helped Rhonda pick up her books. Why, you ask? It's simple.

I am an idiot.

I mean—that's obvious, right? I'm supposed to be winning over the Princesses, not making friends with people they hate. I have a bet to win.

"WHAT'S YOUR NAME?" Rhonda asked me as I helped her to her feet. I will never, ever get used to that screechy voice of hers. Her clothes were even wackier than they had been yesterday. Every single thing she was wearing had an *R* on it.

"I'm Georgia," I told her as I collected her books.
"Georgia Khatchadorian."

"THAT'S BEAUTIFUL!" Rhonda shrieked.

"Um, thanks." I gave her a quick smile and
headed toward my class.

A moment later, I noticed the sound of heavy
breathing behind me.

"SO, GEORGIA, DO YOU LIVE CLOSE TO
HVMS?" Rhonda asked.

"Not that close," I told her. "I have to take a bus."

"I LOVE THE BUS! I HAVE TO TAKE ONE
DOWNTOWN SOMETIMES FOR MY VOICE
LESSONS."

I wasn't really listening. "It's okay, I guess." *Isn't she supposed to be going the other way?*

"DO YOU HAVE ANY BROTHERS OR SISTERS?"

Is she serious? She's never heard of Rafe? Wow, this girl does not get out much. "I've got a brother." I picked up my pace a little, but Rhonda kept up with me. I wondered what would happen if I went into a bathroom. Or oncoming traffic.

"WHAT DO YOU DO FOR FUN, GEORGIA?"

OMG, is she my grandma or something? I wondered. "Well, I'm in a band."

"YOU'RE IN A *BAND*?!?!"

Rhonda said it the way everyone else said, "You're Rafe Khatchadorian's SISTER?!" She sounded shocked. Amazed. Maybe even terrified.

"Yeah. We really...rock." I was going to say "stink," but then I realized that Rhonda would never know the difference.

"OMIGOSH, I WOULD *DIE* TO BE IN A BAND!" Rhonda hugged her books so tightly, I thought they might explode against the ceiling. "I LOVE TO SING!"

I laughed, but then Rhonda looked hurt, and I realized she was serious. "You...sing? You?"

"WHY? DOES YOUR BAND NEED A SINGER?" She grabbed my arm and squeezed it hopefully. And painfully.

"No," I said quickly. "Sorry."

"OH." She looked crestfallen. "BECAUSE I'M REALLY GOOD," Rhonda added.

"Okay," I told her. "Well, here's my class. Gotta go!" And I finally escaped into social studies.

I could feel Rhonda watching me from the door as I sat at my desk. But I didn't look at her. I just stared at the whiteboard until the bell rang and she disappeared.

I am *soooo* regretting being nice to her.

If I'm not careful, she could sink my whole year.

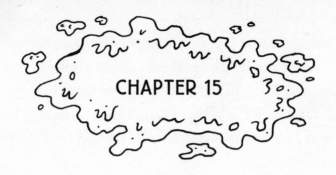

CHAPTER 15

I'm In!

What did I do?

Something. It *had* to be something.

Is it because I took their torture without complaining? Because I ditched the pony backpack? Because I'm the sister of a seriously rebellious HVMS legend who now goes to a totally hip art school?

None of those reasons seemed likely. I only knew one thing: Missy Trillin asked me to have lunch with her and the other Princesses.

There has to be a logical explanation, I thought, but I couldn't figure it out. Here's what happened:

Actually, it was a little more like this:

Ha-ha, ha-ha, Rafe! I'm winning already!

So—okay—maybe they just wanted me to bring them cookies. That was today. Tomorrow, it could be pie. And after a while, I would just be hanging out with them. The fourth Princess, on patrol.

I picked three enormous cookies flecked with M&M's for Missy and the B's. The HVMS cafeteria mostly serves reheated mystery meat, but the desserts are good.

Out in the courtyard, I sat down on a bench, wondering why more people don't eat out there. It was a pretty day, with only a few puffy clouds in a bright blue sky.

"Excuse me?" someone called. It was a cute guy with sandy-blond hair. "Um, hey—" He glanced over his shoulder, then hurried through the cafeteria doors. "You're not supposed to be out here."

"What?" I asked. I turned to look over at the cafeteria windows.

"Oh," I said. I felt like I'd just swallowed a boot: sick and lumpy.

"Are you okay?" the blond kid asked me. "You look like you just swallowed a boot."

Suddenly, the cafeteria doors burst open. In a cloud of smoke, Mrs. Stricker—the Hills Village Middle School vice principal—appeared.

And she was heading straight for us.

CHAPTER 16

Mrs. Stricker Loves Me

Mrs. Stricker swooped toward me. For a moment, I was terrified. Then I remembered something: I had cookies.

"Would you like a cookie, Mrs. Stricker?" I asked in my sweetest voice. "It has M&M's in it." I picked the fattest one from the plate and held it out.

Mrs. Stricker stopped short. She smiled. "You're Georgia Khatchadorian, aren't you?" she asked in a surprisingly gentle voice.

I pointed to him. "This boy has just told me that I'm not supposed to be out in the courtyard. I'm so sorry. I didn't know. I apologize for breaking the rule."

Mrs. Stricker laughed. "Oh, Georgia, don't be

silly. I just came out here to welcome you to Hills Village Middle School."

"Whoa," the blond guy whispered. He stared at me with huge eyes. "Is this, like, some Jedi mind trick thing?"

Impressed, Cute Boy is.

"It's the cookie," I whispered back.

What do they put in these?

"I've seen your permanent record, Georgia,"
Mrs. Stricker went on. "And I know you're a good
student. You even won Most Outstanding Effort in
third grade. I think you've earned the right to eat
where you please."

I had to admit it—I was shocked. Rafe had
always made Mrs. Stricker sound like a witch on
wheels.

"I notice you have two more cookies there." Mrs.
Stricker nodded at the plate on the bench beside
me. "Were you expecting someone else to join you,
Georgia?"

"Oh, no," I lied. "I just…like to give out cookies." I
handed another one to the blond boy.

"Hmm." Mrs. Stricker squinted at the cafeteria
window, where Missy and the B's were cowering
under a table. "I understand what you're going
through, dear," she said. "If there's anything I can
do, Georgia—*anything*—please just come and see
me in my office." She leaned in close and whispered,
"I like to give out cookies too." And then she winked.

CHAPTER 17

Mrs. Stricker Loves Me Not...

Did you buy all that? Yeah, probably not. As soon as I came out of that little daydream, I discovered once again—to my horror—that Rafe was right.

Let me just clear up one thing: Mrs. Stricker is *not* as sweet as an M&M cookie. She's about as sweet as a flaming turd.

Here's the gist of what really happened:

I was still recovering from my humiliation when Mrs. Stricker blazed out to the courtyard. "You aren't supposed to be outside!" she screeched.

"Would you like a cookie?" I asked.

"How *dare* you try to bribe a school official!" I was hoping she would hop on her broomstick and fly away, but instead she snarled, "I know who you are, Rafe Khatchadorian's SISTER! You're breaking a rule—AUTOMATIC DETENTION!"

"Excuse me," the blond boy piped up, "but she didn't know—"

Mrs. Stricker wheeled on him. "Automatic detention for you too, Blond Kid! Nobody covers for a Khatchadorian on my watch!"

CHAPTER 18

"The First Detention Is Always the Hardest" —RAFE K.

I have detention. I, Georgia Khatchadorian, straight-A student and Most Outstanding Effort winner, have detention.

This did not compute, not even when I was sitting in Ms. Donatello's classroom wondering what fresh torture awaited me. What was Rafe going to say?

Come to think of it, he'd probably be *proud*. Ugh!

Ms. Donatello sat behind her desk, looking at me and Sam Marks (Sam is Blond Kid, the random guy who tried to help). Rafe used to call her the Dragon Lady, and I guess she does have a sort of dragonish quality. She seems smart and kind of intimidating. But, also according to Rafe, she's nice.

I guess she falls somewhere between *Eragon* and…well, Puff the Magic Dragon.

| Dangerously Hot | Moderately Toasty | Simply Adorable |

Ms. Donatello interlaced her fingers and looked at me steadily. "Georgia Khatchadorian," she said, leaning forward slightly. "You're Rafe Khatchadorian's sister."

Wow. She didn't even use all caps.

"Yes, I am," I told her. And then, for some unknown reason, I spouted, "Rafe says hi."

Ms. Donatello smiled. "Hello to him. I understand that you're so smart you skipped a grade."

I felt myself blush, and sneaked a look over at Sam, who didn't seem impressed. "Yeah," I said.

Then I let out a little snort of embarrassment, which made me feel like an even bigger dork.

"Are you an artist?" Ms. Donatello asked.

"Uh, I like to draw," I said. I flipped open my notebook and showed her one of my drawings. It happened to be a portrait of Rafe and me—Rafe as a giant blob who's trying to eat me while I fend him off with a sword and a shield.

Ms. Donatello made a little noise as if she were trying to hold back a sneeze. "I see you have a vivid imagination, Georgia," she said. She was struggling with her mouth, but I could tell she wanted to smile. "Sam has a vivid imagination too."

"I'm more of a writer," Sam admitted. "I can't draw at all." His ears turned red.

I wanted to ask him what he liked to write about, but the door flew open. Flames spewed into the classroom. A hideous creature slithered up to Ms. Donatello's desk. "I see you have the perpetrators," Mrs. Stricker said.

"The *students* arrived right on time," Ms. Donatello said. I was starting to see more of her dragon side—the vice principal didn't intimidate her at all.

THE ULTIMATE IMAGINARY CREATURE-TEACHER SMACKDOWN

"Good," Mrs. Stricker snapped. "I'll take over from here."

"I'm usually in charge of detention, Mrs. Stricker."

"Not when there's a Khatchadorian present," Mrs. Stricker snarled. "I have plans for these two." She held up something that looked like a cross between a butter knife and a chisel.

"They can scrape the gum off these desks." Mrs. Stricker smiled. It made her look even scarier than before.

The Dragon Lady huffed out a puff of smoke. I could tell she wanted to say no—but couldn't. She'd lost this round.

So that's how I ended up spending detention with Mrs. Stricker standing over me, watching me remove fossilized gum from the bottoms of booger-encrusted desks.

I ask you: Is life fair?

I answer you: Nope.

I'm a good student. I work hard. I try not to break rules.

Rafe is a bad student. He tried to break every rule in the book. And yet when Rafe got detentions, he would draw and chat with Ms. Donatello. She probably brought doughnuts.

If I ever wanted to get out of here, I was going to have to show Mrs. Stricker that I wasn't a bad kid, like Rafe. I was going to have to get ALL the gum off these desks in record time....

It actually wasn't that hard to hack them off once I pretended each piece was Rafe's head.

A Day at the School Factory

We were halfway through scraping the desks when the school secretary came for Mrs. Stricker. Her husband was on the phone. Surprisingly, Mrs. Stricker dropped everything to go talk to him. Even more surprisingly, someone had married Mrs. Stricker in the first place.

"You two just keep scraping," Mrs. Stricker said. "I'll be back to check on you." She looked right at me when she said that. Then she slithered out the door.

"What did you do to make Stricker love you so much?" Sam whispered once she was gone.

"It's a case of mistaken identity," I told him.

"Right." Sam grinned, like he thought I was joking.

"No, seriously. My brother, Rafe, got detention a lot. So Stricker thinks I must be the same way."

Sam rolled his eyes. "That's pathetic." He chiseled at a chunk of fossilized gum. "But that's how this place works. They treat everyone the same way—like you're a juvenile delinquent waiting to happen."

"Everyone except the Princess Patrol," I corrected.

"Who?"

"Oh—that's what I call Missy Trillin and her friends."

Sam laughed. "I call them the Cheeses."

"Why?"

"Well, because they're cheesy. And because they think they're, like, the Big Cheese. And also because they're so...fake. Like that bright orange spray cheese."

"And yet they rule the school."

"Yeah, Stricker probably wishes we were all like them."

"She'd turn us into them if she could," I agreed. I scraped at yet another chunk of gum, but it wouldn't budge. "Life would be so much easier if I could just fit in," I admitted.

Sam shrugged. "Easier in some ways," he agreed. "Harder in others."

"Harder how?" I asked.

"Fitting in takes a lot of time. Effort. You have to keep trying and trying, and even then it probably isn't going to stick." He shrugged. "Why bother?"

I looked at him with a kind of amazement. How did he understand so much? Sam wore jeans and a rugby shirt. His hair was longish and tousled, and he had two deep dimples that showed when he smiled. He looked like the kind of guy who could fit in anywhere.

He smiled at me, and I smiled back.

And that was when it hit me: Detention with Sam Marks was the best thing that had happened to me since I started middle school.

CHAPTER 20

Every Band Needs a Groupie

We were *jamming*! Detention was over, and the Awesomes were grooving in the garage. We must have been making some amazing noise, because the neighborhood pets were coming to investigate and then howling along. I bet we would have been a hit if we ever got booked to play at the zoo. They say music tames the savage beast, right?

"THAT WAS INCREDIBLE!" Rhonda screeched when the song finished. "CAN I SING WITH YOU GUYS?"

Yes, Rhonda was there. She was standing in front of my garage, waiting, when I got home from detention. True, this afternoon, while we were playing our now-familiar game of Twenty Questions: Rhonda Edition, I might have mentioned that I had rehearsal today. The funny thing is, I don't remember inviting her to watch. Did *you* invite her?

No? Why am I not surprised?

Anyway, there she was. And she wanted to sing.

Mari was looking at me with lifted eyebrows, as if to say *She's* your *friend. What do you think?*

Rhonda was doing her very best impression of a puppy begging for a treat. I swear there were tears in her eyes.

"Um, Rhonda, we really need to practice," I explained.

Rhonda nodded. "OKAY, MAYBE LATER."

"Let's do that last song again," Patti suggested. "I think it's getting there."

We launched into the music. I really gave it all I had, and I think that at least half of the notes were right this time. I've managed to teach myself three chords on the guitar: G, C, and D. It turns out you can use them for almost anything.

We must have been sounding better, because Rhonda started to dance. Well, I *think* she was dancing.

WHICH IS THE CORRECT DESCRIPTION?

a) Rhonda dancing

b) Rhonda being electrocuted

c) Rhonda imitating a chicken

"CAN I SING WITH YOU GUYS NOW?" Rhonda asked once the song was over.

"Well, sure, Rhonda—" Nanci started, but I glared at her and shook my head. She clammed up.

"Rhonda, we're not a karaoke machine," I was explaining just as the breezeway door slammed open. My brother stood there, his fingers plugging his ears.

"Yeah, because a karaoke machine actually sounds like music," Rafe said.

I was about to tell him to get out, when Rhonda *laughed*. I couldn't decide which one of them I wanted to throttle first.

"Get out of here, Rafe!" I shouted.

Nanci sighed as he waved and grinned and scooted back through the door. "We kind of do stink," she admitted.

"I don't think we should sign up for the Battle of the Bands," Mari said.

"Yeah, we'll only embarrass ourselves if we play at your school dance, Georgia," Patti put in.

"ARE YOU KIDDING? YOU GUYS ARE AMAZING!" Rhonda cried. "YOU HAVE TO PLAY THE DANCE!"

Our only groupie, I thought as I watched Rhonda lace her fingers together and beg. I almost wanted to forgive her for laughing at Rafe's joke. (It was a joke, right?)

"Next year," I suggested. "We're not ready yet. But next year we will be."

Mari, Nanci, and Patti looked at one another and nodded. "Yeah," Mari said at last. "Next year we'll really be ready to rock."

I hope, I added, but not out loud.

CHAPTER 21

Squealing on Rafe Is Fun

Mom was home for dinner that night, which meant that dinner would be (a) edible and (b) not my problem, so I had a little time to relax.

I started looking for my copy of *The Book Thief*, but I couldn't find it anywhere. I retraced my steps to the living room, where Rafe was stretched out on the couch. "Rafe, have you seen *The Book Thief*?"

"Nope."

"What's that in your hand?"

"This?" Rafe flipped closed the book he was holding and frowned at the cover. "*The Book Thief*." He went back to reading.

Reading! What the heck? Rafe doesn't read!

I planted one hand on my hip and held out the other. "Give it."

"You know what I like about this book?" Rafe asked casually.

"No…"

"Give me that!" I said, grabbing the book out of his hands. "Mom!" I could hear Rafe laughing as I stomped into the kitchen, fuming.

"What is it, honey?" Mom looked up from the carrots she was chopping, and I noticed that she seemed tired.

"Rafe stole my book," I reported.

"Rafe?" Mom's face brightened with a smile. "He wanted to read your book?"

Ugh—this isn't going well, I thought. I decided to change tactics. "Rafe has about six months' worth of old, used chewing gum stuck all over his room."

"What?" Mom put down the knife.

"Rafe is hoarding old gum," I told her. "He even keeps some in the toilet!"

That did it.

"Rafe!" Mom shouted, and stomped out of the kitchen. I could practically see the steam coming from her ears.

Ha! Revenge is sweet. Or in Rafe's case, old and sticky.

CHAPTER 22

My Mom Is My Worst Nightmare

The bad news: Jules doesn't like it when I squeal on Rafe, but sometimes I just can't help myself. So after she collared Rafe, she sent me to my room.

That wasn't a big surprise.

The good news: Sound travels really well from Rafe's room to mine, so I could hear every word of Mom's shriek-fest at Rafe. Also—I had popcorn!

Is it sad that this is the best part of my day?

Better than reality TV!

Wow—Mom's investigation into Rafe's chewing gum "collection" was really thorough. She even found the gum I'd hidden in his sock drawer!

Rafe was furious, of course. He denied that the gum was his, which only made Mom angrier.

It was fun while it lasted. Unfortunately, it lasted only seven minutes. Then Mom came to my room.

I stashed the popcorn under my bed as she opened my door and then closed it softly behind her. Next, she took a deep breath, almost a sigh, and looked at me. "The school called earlier," she said.

"Oh." It was as if frost had settled on my clothes—the chill ran down to my bones. "Um—what about?"

"About your detention."

"I was going to tell you—" She held up her hand, and I clamped my lips together. "Sorry," I murmured.

Mom sat at the foot of my bed and ran her fingers through her blond hair. "Georgia, you know that Rafe made a lot of mistakes at Hills Village," she began.

They weren't mistakes.

"I'm not like him," I said quickly.

"I just don't want you to go through what he went through." Mom's eyes teared up a little, and I felt *awful. This is worse than getting yelled at*, I realized. I've always tried to be the kid Mom doesn't have to worry about. I would have given anything to trade places with Rafe at that moment. I'd rather have Mom mad at me than have her disappointed in me.

What kind of world is it when Rafe is reading for fun and I'm making Mom cry by being in detention?

"I'll never get detention again," I promised. "I *won't.*"

"I'm glad to hear it, honey," Mom said, squeezing my hand.

I swear, I never meant to break my promise so fast.

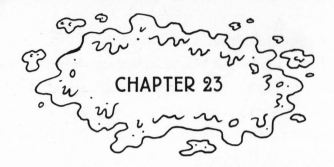

CHAPTER 23

It Ain't Easy Being Green

I adjusted the towel on my head and frowned at the outfit I'd just laid out on my bed. *Which is safer?* I wondered. *Jeans or leggings?*

I decided to go with the jeans and a plain red shirt, no logo. *Don't give the Princesses anything to pick on*, I thought.

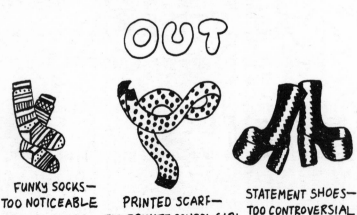

FUNKY SOCKS—
TOO NOTICEABLE

PRINTED SCARF—
TOO PRIVATE-SCHOOL GIRL

STATEMENT SHOES—
TOO CONTROVERSIAL

UNSCENTED DEODORANT

CLOAK OF INVISIBILITY

I pulled on my "safe" outfit and found a pair of plain brown socks. I slipped my feet into a pair of low black boots. Then it was time to dry my hair.

No braids, I thought. *No gel. Just plain.* I took the towel off my head.

GREEN HAIR!

"Rafe!" I screamed, practically flying down the stairs and into the kitchen. "That's it! That's IT!"

Rafe cracked up. Mom stepped between us, which was lucky—for Rafe.

"Oh, green hair!" Grandma Dotty said cheerfully. "Very daring, Georgia! I *love* punk rock!"

"Rafe, are you responsible for this?" Mom asked.

"Absolutely," Rafe said between snickers.

"I'm going to shove that cereal spoon up your nose and into your brain!" I screeched at my brother. My wet, scraggly green hair dripped into my eyes.

"Worth it!" Rafe crowed. "You look like you've got seaweed on your head!"

"Why would you do something like this?" Mom demanded.

"Georgia knows why," Rafe snapped. He flashed me an evil, triumphant grin.

"This is very serious, Rafe," Mom said.

A flash of guilt passed across my brother's face. He doesn't like disappointing her either. "It'll wash out..." he said. "After a while."

"How long?" I demanded.

"A week?"

"Mom!" I screamed.

"Rafe, I don't have time to deal with you this morning. But you will be punished for this." She turned to me and put a gentle hand on my shoulder. "Georgia, maybe you can wear a hat or something."

"How about a paper bag over her head?" Rafe suggested.

Mom glared at him, and he clamped his mouth shut.

No hats, I thought grimly. "I'll just suffer."

"Rock the Casbah!" Grandma Dotty shouted.

I had no idea what that "casbah" thing was about, but somehow I got the message. *Mission: Blend In* was terminated. I needed to buck up and steel myself for whatever was next.

Rock on!

CHAPTER 24

The Princesses' Hairstyle Rules

I got a lot of stares the minute I walked through the double doors. Not surprising. Grandma Dotty had been so enthusiastic about the "punk" style I was rocking that I decided I might as well play it up. Before I left the apartment, I'd pulled my hair back with a sparkly barrette.

I spotted Rhonda at her locker, so I put my face down and steered in the other direction. Not to be mean—I just didn't feel like answering ten zillion questions about my hair. But with my head down like that, I nearly ran right into someone else.

"Sorry," I said as I swerved to avoid slamming into Sam Marks.

He stopped in his tracks. "Wow!" he said when he realized it was me, which made me blush. "You look like…" He trailed off, shaking his head. "Like a leaf…with sparkly dew on it."

"Um, thanks." I hadn't been expecting a compliment—at least, I thought it was a compliment—and didn't really know how to handle it. "You look nice too," I said, which didn't make any sense at all. He was just wearing a T-shirt and jeans.

And then I heard the voice I'd been expecting—and dreading.

"Oh my gawd!" Missy screeched. "She went from Weedwacker to weed!"

Okay, so even though I knew I looked like I was about to start sprouting dandelions, the dig still really hurt, coming from Missy.

I cringed as the Princesses surrounded me. "Now her hair matches her face—ugly," Brittany said.

"I thought her hairstyle was bad before," Bethany agreed.

"Cut it out, you guys," Sam said, which made me squirm even more than the insults did. I didn't want him to hear this.

But Missy just ignored him. She pursed her lips.

"She's having a bad hair year."

Do they rehearse this stuff at home?

Then Missy got a really smug little smile on her face. It was a smile I did not like at all. "Not only is her hair ugly," she said dramatically, "it's just really *limp*."

The other Princesses cracked up while I fought back tears. My face burned, and my blood boiled like acid through my whole body. I felt like I was going to dissolve.

"Shut up!" Sam shouted.

Missy stared at him. I stared at him. I think *everyone* was staring at him.

"You think you're so great, Missy," Sam went on. "But everyone just hates your guts!"

Well, it wasn't quite like that. It was more like this:

Missy tossed her hair and said, "Oh, did you overhear that, Sam?" she asked. "It must be because your ears are so big."

Sam shook his head at her, like she was an annoying piece of toilet paper that kept getting stuck to his shoe, no matter what he did. Then he turned to me. "Are you okay?" he asked gently.

I tried to talk. I really tried. I opened my mouth. I licked my lips. But nothing would come out. Somehow, Sam being nice to me made the Princesses' meanness worse, and I couldn't take it. I just couldn't.

And so I ran.

CHAPTER 25

I Wasn't Crying About My Hair

I didn't care about my green hair. Well, okay, I didn't care about it *much*.

It's the other stuff I couldn't stand.

You're confused—I can tell. Look, there might be one or two things I've left out of this book so far. I guess I've never mentioned that one of my legs is shorter than the other. I wear a special shoe, which helps, but I still limp a little.

Get it?

Your hair is **LIMP.**

Your personality is **LAME.**

You're a **DRAG.**

Pretty hilarious, right?

And "clip-clop"? That's the way the Princesses made fun of the sound my feet make when I walk. I'm a little uneven, I guess.

I actually got the joke the first time they said it. But I guess I didn't feel like explaining it. You understand, don't you? It's not like I'm a liar.

(What? Rafe never mentioned my shoe either? Well, that's…interesting.)

Nobody at my old school even noticed my limp. Well, if they noticed, at least they never really cared. I mean, sometimes, of course, it came up. Like, I always got picked last when we had relay races.

But that didn't happen all that often. All in all, I really never thought about it much. Everyone was just used to me, and they accepted me.

But middle school was totally different. The more I tried to blend in, the more I stood out. It's like I was some kind of free entertainment that people couldn't help but stare at. *Free freak show! See the Limpy Chick in her natural habitat! Mock her hair! Judge her clothes! Remember her crazy brother?*

So is it a surprise that I was locked in a

bathroom stall, crying? (I'm telling you, middle school is all glamour.) I blew my nose on a strip of toilet paper and took a shaky breath.

I wondered if I could just stay in this stall forever. With wireless Internet access, I might never have to face the world again.

CHAPTER 26

I'm Being Followed

ARE YOU OKAY?"

Rhonda was standing in front of the row of sinks with a roll of toilet paper in her hand when I finally got the will to leave the bathroom stall. What a surprise.

I heaved a sigh, which came out as a hiccup. I couldn't decide whether I was happy to see her or annoyed that she'd followed me into the bathroom. Both, I guess.

"I'm fine, thanks." I took the roll of toilet paper and tore off a half dozen squares. My nose was really runny.

I checked myself out in the mirror as I splashed water on my face and patted it dry with a scratchy brown paper towel. I looked pretty hideous. Green hair, red and splotchy face…I looked like something out of a Muppets movie.

Rhonda patted me on the back as I headed toward the door. I appreciated the silent support. Unfortunately, the silence ended the minute we stepped into the hallway.

"I REALLY LOVE YOUR HAIR! WHAT MADE YOU DECIDE TO DYE IT GREEN?"

I snorted. "It was my brother's idea." It was funny how people—except the Princesses—seemed to like the green hair. Maybe Rafe wasn't so crazy after all.

"ARE YOU GOING TO KEEP IT GREEN?" Rhonda asked. "YOU REALLY SHOULD! IT'S

AWESOME FOR A ROCK STAR! OR MAYBE YOU'LL TRY A FEW DIFFERENT COLORS? DO YOU THINK YOU MIGHT GO FOR PURPLE?"

It was kind of amazing how quickly Rhonda could think of new questions. She didn't even need answers.

"IT'S SO GREAT THAT YOU AREN'T AFRAID TO HAVE GREEN HAIR," Rhonda gushed. "YOU AND I ARE A LOT ALIKE—WE'RE NOT AFRAID TO BE DIFFERENT, RIGHT, GEORGIA?"

Rhonda was talking at an even higher volume than usual, and a few people stared as we made our way down the hall. "I'm not trying to be different," I snapped.

"YOU'RE JUST BEING YOURSELF!" Rhonda crowed. "WE ARE WHO WE ARE!"

"Rhonda! We're *not* alike, okay?" I snarled in a tone I usually save for Rafe. "So can you please just stop following me around?"

Rhonda froze up. Her eyes filled with tears.

I am the worst person ever, I thought. Yelling at Rhonda is like yelling at a puppy that just can't help itself. "I'm sorry, Rhonda—I'm just…"

Her face brightened. "YOU'RE JUST HAVING A BAD DAY!"

"Yeah," I told her. "I am. I didn't mean to take it out on you."

"IT'S OKAY," Rhonda said. "IT HAPPENS TO EVERYONE. DO YOU KNOW WHAT HAPPENED TO ME ONCE? I ACCIDENTALLY STUFFED MY SKIRT INTO MY UNDERPANTS AND..."

She kept talking all the way down the hall.

Like I said, she just can't help herself.

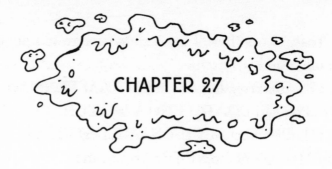

CHAPTER 27

Stop, Book Thief!

A miracle!

I sat in homeroom for fifteen minutes, and NOTHING horrible happened.

Mr. Grank didn't even mention my hair, which made me wonder if he's color-blind. It would definitely explain some of his outfits.

Then the bell rang for first period. It was about time for something horrible to happen, right? I was three steps from the door when Mini-Miller swiped my book right out from under my arm.

"That's what you get for walking so slow, Peg Leg." He grinned his dumb grin at me.

"Do you even read?"

Mini-Miller shrugged his enormous shoulders. "No."

I planted my hands on my hips. "So, what are you going to do with a copy of *The Book Thief*?"

Mini-Miller snorted. "Duh," he said. "Sell it on eBay."

Great. Mini-Miller will probably be the next Internet millionaire, thanks to me.

Big Money magazine

Bully your way to success!

Rafe Khatchadorian and the Great Zoom Scam

Tax Evasion 101

I sighed and watched Mini-Miller lope down the hallway. I couldn't believe my copy of *The Book Thief* was stolen by a real book thief. Could this day get any worse?

Yes, it could!

Because just at the moment Mini-Miller turned the corner, Mrs. Stricker swooped past him going in the other direction—toward *me*.

The minute she saw my hair, her face lit up. I could tell I'd just made her day. Not in a good way.

"Green hair, Rafe Khatchadorian's SISTER?!" she screeched. "That's a violation of our dress code! I'll see you in detention!"

And she took off down the hallway, gleefully passing out a stack of brand-new *HVMS Code of Conduct* booklets.

CHAPTER 28

My Six Favorite Books This Year (So Far)

Who wants to give the first oral book report?"

Before the question was out of Mr. Mahoney's mouth, my hand shot into the air. Teachers are always impressed when you show enthusiasm— and I wanted to prove that I was no Rafe Khatchadorian! Mrs. Stricker might have just accused me of a genetic relationship, but none of my *real* teachers had called me Rafe in more than a week. By the time I finished my oral report, that name would be wiped from everyone's memory— permanently.

"Does anyone *else* wish to go first?" Mr. Mahoney asked. "Anyone?"

I left my hand in the air and looked around. Nobody else was moving.

Mr. Mahoney let out a huge sigh. "All right, Ms. Khatchadorian," he said. "You may proceed."

I carried my stack of books (minus one) to the

front of the room and cleared my throat. "I know we're only supposed to give a report on one book," I said with a smile, "but I couldn't decide which was my favorite, so I narrowed it down to my top six...."

"You have only five books," Mr. Mahoney pointed out.

"One of them was stolen," I explained. *"The Book Thief."*

Mr. Mahoney frowned. "Is that a joke? Are you trying to be funny, Ms. Khatchadorian?"

"Um, no. Unfortunately." This wasn't going well. I decided to switch gears. "I'd like to start my report by reciting a poem that's in *The Outsiders*. It's by Robert Frost." I knelt down and stuck out my arms to look like flower petals. "'Nature's first green is gold,'" I quoted. "'Her hardest hue to'—"

Mr. Mahoney interrupted me. "Did you dye your hair green for this presentation? To go with that poem?"

"Um, yes?" I heard a few snickers, but I didn't mind. I'd rather have people think I dyed my hair to get an A in English than have people think I was the victim of a prank. Or think I did it to be cool. Because it definitely *wasn't* cool.

"I've heard enough," Mr. Mahoney said. "Sit down."

"What?" I blinked in surprise. *Does he mean my report is so amazing I don't even need to finish?*

"You Khatchadorians think you can turn everything into a big joke," Mr. Mahoney growled. He scribbled in his notebook. "Your grade is a D."

For a moment I couldn't move. D. He gave me a D. I'd *never* gotten below a B+ in my *entire life*!

"Please sit down, Ms. Khatchadorian," he repeated.

"But you haven't even heard my report," I said.

"Sit. Down."

I didn't have much choice. So I took my books and sat down.

I'd tried to erase Rafe's name from everyone's memory, but I'd only managed to carve it deeper in stone. Somehow, I was able to keep from crying. That was the only thing that went right that morning.

CHAPTER 29

The Truth About Jeanne Galletta

After school Mrs. Stricker sent me to the cafeteria for detention, where Mr. Adell, the janitor, was waiting with a bucket full of bacteria and a sponge.

"You're supposed to wipe down the tables," he said, handing me the sponge.

"What's in there?" I asked, looking at the bucket.

"Water and disinfectant," Mr. Adell said.

That wasn't what it smelled like, but I had to take his word for it. I started in on the tables. They were even grosser than the desks had been. Did you know that ketchup can get stuck to a table like glue? Did you realize that a spilled smoothie turns into an oozy jelly? Or that chocolate milk will become a solid if left out all day? Neither did I!

How very educational.

What could be worse than spending time with bacteria?

Having Missy Trillin watch me spend time with bacteria. She and her sidekicks sat huddled in one corner of the lunchroom, planning the school dance. They were listening to an eighth grader lay out the plans for decorations and refreshments. When I heard Missy say the older girl's name, I stopped in my tracks.

When Rafe was at HVMS, he had an imaginary friend. Of course, I am talking about none other than Jeanne Galletta. Oh, she's real, all right—*and she was sitting with Missy at that very moment*. But I don't think she and Rafe were really friends. I know for sure that Rafe would've liked to be *better* friends with Jeanne. He was always saying that Jeanne was so sweet and kind and smart and hardworking and well dressed (like he would know). I figured I'd spot Jeanne on my very first day at HVMS, floating down from the ceiling with white robes fluttering around her, strumming a harp and showing off her glowing halo.

But it turns out that Jeanne must just be a regular eighth grader, because I never would've picked her out of a lineup.

Jeanne just sat there, talking to the Princesses like they were normal people. *Maybe they're her friends*, I thought as I cleaned a table in the far corner. Missy said something, and the others—even Jeanne— laughed. *Are they giggling about me?* I wondered. *Even perfect Jeanne Galletta is picking on me now.*

I went to find Mr. Adell. "I'm finished," I told him, holding out the bucket.

"Did you clean that one?" he asked, pointing to the table where the Princesses sat. I could feel their glares from across the room.

My stomach did a flip, then tied itself into a knot. "No."

He shrugged. "Then you're not done."

I gulped. *This detention is cruel and unusual punishment*, I thought as I dragged myself over to the Princesses.

"What do you want?" Missy demanded.

"I'm supposed to wipe down your table," I said, holding up my bucket.

"Ew," Missy said. "What's that—your shampoo?" Brittany and Bethany howled as if that was the best joke in the history of humankind. Even Jeanne laughed.

She laughed! *Where's your angel now, Rafe?* I thought. I should have known he had rotten taste in girls.

"I *like* your green hair," Jeanne said.

Missy smiled smugly. "Yeah, it's very eco-friendly."

"The alien look is totally in," Brittany agreed.

"Beam me up, Georgia," Bethany added. Missy gave her a high five.

Great. Now there were *four* princesses instead of three. Even more witty remarks to ruin my life! "Can I just clean this table?" I snapped.

"We'll move," Jeanne said, gathering her things. "Let's sit over there," she said, pointing to a table by the window. "The only thing left to plan is the Battle of the Bands."

The itty-bitty dance committee looked at one another, then gathered their things to follow. I guess even Missy wasn't going to mess with Jeanne.

Is there a new queen at HVMS? I wondered.

I turned my back on them as I wiped down my last table. *Why did Rafe ever like Jeanne, anyway? She's just like the rest of them—underneath that bouncy hair, she has a mean streak a mile wide.*

General Rafe Torture

I couldn't let the green-hair thing go. I needed revenge.

I know what you're thinking: "Sheesh, Georgia's been a little harsh on Rafe, hasn't she?" Yeah. I have. But you need to understand something: *He ruined my life.* I had always loved school. I'd always been good at it. And now it was *horrible*, and it was all Rafe's fault.

He was my brother, and I was stuck with him... but he was stuck with me too. And I would make him pay. I rubbed my hands together like an evil mad scientist. (Hey, I already had the hair to match.)

When I came into the kitchen, Rafe was there,

chugging milk straight from the plastic jug. Seriously. *Again* with the chugging!

From the Mind of *Georgia Khatchadorian*

Reminder! Never drink milk again.

I bit back a comment about backwash and picked an apple out of the fruit bowl. "Hey, you got a phone call earlier," I said, like the thought had just occurred to me.

Rafe looked stumped, as if I had just told him a riddle. "Who?"

"Oh…wait…I can't remember her name." I took a bite of the apple, pretending to rack my brain.

Rafe's eyes bugged out when I said "her." "Someone from Airbrook?"

BWA-HA-HA HA-HA! Sucker!

"No…it was someone from HVMS," I said. "Someone who used to know you."

"Jeanne Galletta?"

I snapped my fingers. "That's it. Sorry I didn't write it down. She said you had the number?"

Rafe looked thrilled, as if I'd just told him Santa Claus was real and he was coming over for dinner.

Rafe grabbed the phone from the wall and started to punch in the numbers. *He has her number memorized?* I don't think he even realized how huge his smile was. Rafe was happier than I'd seen him in weeks.

And that was when I knew that this was really mean. Too mean. Meaner than turning someone's hair green.

"Wait—" I said. I didn't want to be an evil mad scientist.

"Hey, Jeanne?" Rafe grinned. "Hey, it's Rafe!" There was a pause. "Yeah, that Rafe." Another pause. His smile faltered a bit. "Well…I called because I heard you left a message earlier.…" My brother looked at me, clearly confused. "Oh. Oh, yeah. Of course not. It, uh, must have been Jeanne from my new school.…" He gave a fake little laugh, but his face was so red I thought it might melt off.

He glared in my direction. *Yikes.* I wanted to tell him I was sorry, but he was still on the phone with Jeanne.

"Oh, yeah, I really like Airbrook Arts," Rafe said cheerfully into the receiver. *Watch out*, he mouthed at me, eyes narrowed. "How's HVMS? What are you up to?" Then he turned his back on me and started toward the stairs. I heard him slam the door to his bedroom.

I looked down at my apple. I'd only taken one bite, but I didn't want it anymore.

It ain't easy being mean.

CHAPTER 31

Rafe's Revenge

GEORGIA! GEORGIA, CONGRATULATIONS!"
Rhonda screeched as I walked into HVMS five days
later.

It wasn't even first period, and I already
had no idea what was going on. "What are you
congratulating me for?"

"THE LIST FOR BATTLE OF THE BANDS IS
UP—AND YOUR BAND IS ON IT!" She grabbed
my arms and shook me. "YOU'RE GOING TO
PERFORM AT THE DANCE!"

"WHAT?" I shrieked. For once, my voice was as
loud as Rhonda's. "Are you sure?"

Rhonda pointed, and I dashed over to the display case in the school lobby. Here's what I saw:

BATTLE OF THE BANDS!
PERFORMANCE BEGINS AT 7:30!

1. **FURRY BURPS** (Tom Manderly, Ahmed Usman, Jill West)
4. **LADY DADA** (Allison Vidder)
5. **DERANGED LUNCH LADY** (DeVaughn Green, Pete Baker)
6. **WE STINK** (Nanci Ricci, Mari Alvarez, Patti Bahrey, Georgia Khatchadorian)

"We can't play the dance!" I wailed. "How did this happen?" And then, like lightning striking, I realized two things:

1. Only one person calls my band We Stink.
2. That person was recently on the phone with Jeanne Galletta, head of the dance committee.

He got me. Rafe got me in my own school. He was going to make sure I humiliated myself in front of everyone.

"YOU'RE GOING TO BE AMAZING!" Rhonda gushed.

This doesn't even have anything to do with you! I wanted to shout. But I didn't. Instead, I sat down right there, in the middle of the floor.

"ARE YOU OKAY?" Rhonda plopped down next to me.

"Rhonda—we can't play the dance! We really do stink. We're not ready!" I buried my head in my arms. "What am I going to tell the band?"

Rhonda sat there for a long time, not saying anything. That was so unusual that I actually peeked out from behind my arms, just to make sure she was still breathing.

She was. In fact, she was watching me and smiling. Sometime while I had my head in my arms, she had already managed to make a sign that read WE STINK RULES! She put a gentle hand on my shoulder.

"YOU CAN TELL THE BAND," she said seriously, "TO GET READY TO ROCK."

CHAPTER 32

Playing War

Mom and Rafe were playing cards in the living room when I got home from school. Rafe looked up from his hand and narrowed his eyes at me. "What's new, Georgia?" he asked.

I snorted. "You already know what's new, Rafe." I nearly tripped over the pile of mail in the front hall. *Am I the only one who picks things up around here?* I thought as I gathered up the mess and sorted through it.

Mom slapped down a card, then Rafe did the same. "Ha!" Rafe said, greedily snapping up the pair and kissing it with a gross, wet smack. I thought I saw the jack of clubs get a little green in the face.

Mom laughed. "How was your day, sweetheart?" she asked as I hung my coat on a peg in the hall and walked over to the couch.

"Fine," I said sweetly. I held up a treasure I'd just found in the pile of mail. "Look, Rafe! It's from Airbrook Arts! Did you get progress reports already?" I smile at him. "I wonder how you did!"

"Give me that!" Rafe snarled, reaching for the envelope.

I yanked it away. "I bet you can't wait to open it up and see!"

Get ready for smackage!

Bzzzzz

Bzzz

Mom stood up. "I'll take that, Georgia," she said, and I handed it to her.

Rafe glowered at me as Mom tore off the end of the envelope and pulled out the report. Her eyes went wide. "Rafe!" she shouted. "You did great!" Mom wrapped Rafe in a huge hug. "Look at this! An A in art! And all the rest are B's!"

Rafe looked down at the paper, as if he could hardly believe it himself. "I'm getting a C in math," he pointed out.

"A C-plus," Mom corrected. "You'll pull it up—I know you will! Oh, Rafe!" She squeezed him tight. "I'm so proud of you!" Mom dabbed at her eyes a little bit. Seriously, I hadn't seen her this happy since the time she found a ten-dollar bill at the playground.

"I'm making pie to celebrate," Mom announced, and started for the kitchen.

"Apple?" Rafe asked, padding after her.

I watched them go. *Well, that backfired big-time.* Rafe was actually doing well in school, while I'm working on a D in English.

Welcome to my alternate universe.

CHAPTER 33

Shoo Pie, Don't Bother Me

I stomped to my bedroom, flopped onto my bed, and recapped everything that had gone wrong in the past few days. Green hair and detention were just two of the highlights. And now...Rafe revenge reversal. *Mom is baking him a pie!* I still couldn't believe it.

There was a soft knock at my door. *Rafe*, I thought. *He's come to gloat.* "Go away."

"What did you say, Carolina?" Grandma Dotty asked as she opened the door. "'Slow decay'?"

"No, I—never mind. Come on in."

Grandma Dotty sat down at the foot of my bed and rubbed my back for a minute. Mom used to do that when I was little. I forgot how nice it could feel. "What's wrong, honey?"

"Nothing."

"Hmm. Then why are you lying facedown on your bed?"

Sighing, I sat up. "It's just—Rafe got his progress report today. He got one lousy A, and Mom is acting like he just got into college. He even got a C! Do you know what would happen if I got a C?"

And it's coconut cream. I **hate** coconut.

Dotty clapped. "An A is marvelous!"

"But I get straight A's all the time!" I wailed. "And Mom never made me a pie!"

Grandma Dotty looked thoughtful. "She never made me a pie for my report card either."

What? Mom wasn't even alive when Grandma got her report card. *Well, maybe that's Dotty's point—that life isn't fair.*

"I want pie too," I grumbled.

"Well, maybe Rafe will let you have some." Dotty smiled and took my hand in her wrinkly old one. I knew she was trying to help, but she wasn't really getting my point. "It's good that your brother is doing well in art school," Dotty went on. "He's never been the greatest student, you know."

"Tell me about it." I rolled my eyes.

"He's like your mother in that way. They're both born artists. They aren't much good at regular school. They're a lot alike, in good ways and bad." Grandma Dotty smiled, and her brown eyes twinkled.

"Am I like my mom?" I asked. "Like she used to be?" I was hoping Dotty would say that both Mom and I were smart. Or musical. Or kind, maybe.

Dotty shrugged. "How should I know?" she asked. "I don't know what your mother was like when she was your age."

What? She doesn't know my mom?

I wanted to say it out loud, but I thought it might be kinda cruel. I mean, Dotty's memory is kind of Swiss cheesy. There are holes. There's nothing she can do about it. Why make her feel worse?

Let's face it: That's what makes Grandma Dotty a little…dotty. Or more like completely dotty. And we all love her anyway.

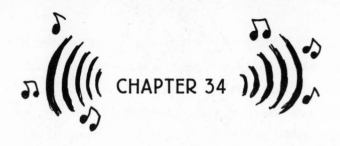

CHAPTER 34

Completely Insane

I have to tell them, I thought as my fingers plucked the strings of my electric guitar. *I have to tell them. I'll tell them right after this song.*

The song ended. I didn't tell them.

Mari, Nanci, and Patti still had no idea that Rafe had signed us up for the Battle of the Bands yesterday. I wished I could put off telling them forever, but I knew I couldn't. For one thing, Rhonda was watching our rehearsal, and she was *dying* to tell my friends about our upcoming "gig."

More like a gag.

If I didn't say anything, I knew Rhonda would. And that wouldn't be pretty.

Okay, I couldn't let that happen.

"I'm beat," Mari announced when the next song ended.

"Yeah, I have to get home," Patti added, wrapping a scarf around her neck. "Mom needs me to mow the lawn."

"So, we'll rehearse again next week?" Nanci asked. She shoved her drumsticks into her back pocket and dug her hand into a bag of chips. "Same time, same place?"

Rhonda gaped at me. *TELL THEM!* she mouthed.

"Wait," I said. My friends turned to look at me.

"What's up, Georgia?" Mari asked.

"Um..." The only way to say it was to spew it. "Rafe signed us up for the Battle of the Bands which is in eight days so we have to practice because we'll be performing in front of the whole school and our names are already on the program so it's kind of too late to back out but I probably could if we really wanted to so it's up to you guys." I squeezed my eyes shut.

"What?" Nanci asked. She crunched a chip.

"We're signed up to do the Battle of the Bands?" Patti asked. She made it sound like *You volunteered us to jump off a bridge?*

Nanci and Mari looked at each other. It was a look of horror.

"Our names are on the program?" Mari asked.

"Rafe did it," I said.

Dead silence.

I wish I could just dig a hole and live in it, I thought. *Maybe Mom could bring me a sandwich now and then.*

"COME ON, YOU GUYS!" Rhonda screeched. "THIS IS GOING TO BE AWESOME!"

"Rhonda, we're not ready," Mari pointed out.

"YOU *ARE* READY! YOU'RE AMAZING, AND THE DANCE WILL BE PATHETIC WITHOUT YOU!" She waved her arms in the air. "YOU OWE IT TO GEORGIA TO PERFORM! YOU CAN'T BACK OUT ON HER IN FRONT OF HER FRIENDS."

I put up my hands. "Wait! This doesn't really have anything to do with me—"

"YOU GUYS WILL REGRET IT FOREVER IF YOU BACK OUT NOW," Rhonda insisted. "HOW WILL YOU PERFORM NEXT YEAR IF YOU BAIL ON THIS YEAR'S BATTLE?"

Mari turned to Patti. "Rhonda has a point."

She does?

"SO WHAT IF YOU'RE NOT PERFECT?" Rhonda was clearly in the zone. She wasn't about to stop screeching now. "ROCK IS NEVER PERFECT!"

"She's right!" Nanci twirled a drumstick. "Let's rock!"

"Yeah, let's go for it!" Patti agreed.

Mari turned to me. "What do you think, Georgia?"

I looked over at Rhonda's beaming face. *She really, really thinks we're good*, I realized. It was kind of inspiring.

"Let's do it," I said.

Rhonda let out a shriek that might have been a cheer. I clapped my hands over my ears but smiled. Rhonda was our biggest fan, and I didn't want to let her down.

Of course, she might just be completely insane.

But I didn't want to let her down anyway.

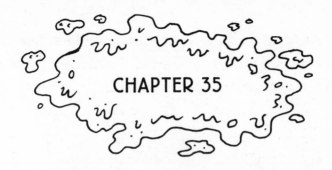

CHAPTER 35

Grandma's Nineteenth Nervous Breakdown

I was almost home from school when I saw him: Rafe.

We had managed to avoid each other in the morning. Airbrook Arts starts forty-five minutes later than HVMS, so I ate a piece of pie for breakfast and snuck out early. But I couldn't avoid him forever.

Rafe had paused midstride too. For a moment, we both stood stock-still, like mirror images. I guess we were both waiting for the other to make the first move.

I knew the same question was on both of our
minds: *Who's going to pull the next prank?*

True, I had pulled the last one. And yet that
prank was an epic fail for me, and a big, fat win for
Rafe. So whose turn was it? Would the next victim
be Rafe? Or me?

"What are you planning?" Rafe demanded.

"Nothing," I said. "You?"

"Nothing."

His hands were empty, so I decided to trust him.

I guess Rafe made the same decision about me, because he nodded, and we started up the walk to our house. We walked up the steps. Rafe opened the door....

Wait—is this the right house?

"Surprise!" Grandma Dotty cried. She was sitting on a hideous flowered couch. "I got my things out of storage and decided to freshen up the decor around here."

It wasn't that our apartment looked awful.... It was just that it looked exactly like Dotty's old house. I looked at Rafe. Rafe looked at me.

"This is bad," Rafe whispered.

"Wait till you see what I've done with the other rooms!" Dotty chuckled.

"Other rooms?" Rafe repeated, but I was already racing up the stairs. I threw open the door to my personal space.

"What's this?" I shrieked. "Where's my stuff?" My room now had a couch, a plant, and an empty birdcage. I yanked open the closet. Nothing. "Where's Mr. Bananas?" My stuffed monkey had disappeared, along with my Most Outstanding Effort medal, my favorite blanket, and my *bed*.

I heard Rafe howl next door and raced to see the destruction there.

"This looks way better than it used to," I told him.

"It's horrible!" Rafe cried. "I can't find anything! Where's my favorite drawing pen? Where's the painting Mom made for me? Where's last Thursday's leftover pizza? This room is about as fun as… a prison cell."

"This is a disaster!" Rafe wailed. "That pizza was my science project!"

"We have to tell Grandma to put everything back where it was," I said.

"She probably has no clue how to do that," Rafe pointed out. "And she might not want to. She's kind of…" His voice trailed off.

"Dotty?" I suggested.

"Exactly."

We needed to come up with a way to make Dotty *want* to give us back our stuff. Suddenly, it came to me.

"Listen, Rafe," I said, taking him by the shoulder. "I have a plan. But I'm going to need your help."

Rafe looked suspicious. "What's the plan?"

"We have to convince Grandma to get all our old stuff out from wherever she put it," I said. "Let's tell her we'll have a garage sale. Then she'll put everything out, and we'll sort through it and keep what we really want before we sell anything."

"Grandma Dotty goes to garage sales every Sunday," Rafe said. "She can't resist them." He took a deep breath. "Okay, Georgia," he said finally, "you can count on me."

CHAPTER 36

"We Stink" Up the Garage Sale

I don't think I've *ever* worn this coat," Grandma Dotty said as she put a $3.00 sticker on a purple quilted jacket. "No wonder we have a closet full of clutter!"

"Actually, Grandma, that's my coat," I said, plucking the sticker from the sleeve.

"No wonder it's so small!" Dotty grinned and moved on to a blue-and-gray-striped winter hat. "Oh, this has *got* to go."

I was being Super Sister, so I rescued the hat, which was Rafe's. So far, he'd been pretty helpful with the garage sale. The good news: Most of our belongings had reappeared over the weekend. The bad news: Dotty kept getting confused and putting price tags on them. We had to act fast, or our friends and neighbors would be wearing our clothes and snuggling our stuffed animals. But Dotty was having a ball with the tags—she'd even stuck one on the straw hat she was wearing. So I was trying to rescue only things we really needed, like winter clothes and moldy science projects.

I was—as Dotty says—making orange juice from lemons.

No, *literally*. I was making orangeade. I'd read on a website that giving away drinks and snacks at a garage sale puts people in a good mood and makes them want to buy stuff.

"Where does this go?" Rafe asked as he lugged a telephone table out onto the lawn.

"Let's put it toward the front," I told him. "We can display my old ceramic-cat collection on it."

"You're getting rid of that?" Rafe looked surprised. "I always kind of liked it."

"You did?" Wow, that was a shock. Rafe used to tease me about it constantly.

"Yeah, it made it easy to buy you Christmas presents." Rafe shrugged. "Oh, well." I was touched as he hauled the table away.

I always knew he liked us.

Did you forget how he smashed Mittens?

Is it possible, I thought, *that my brother isn't so bad after all?*

"HEY, GEORGIA! I'M HERE TO HELP WITH THE GARAGE SALE!" Beaming, Rhonda grabbed a glass of orangeade. "WOW! THIS IS SO REFRESHING!"

"Um, hey, Rhonda." I had no idea how she'd even found out about the garage sale. *Is she psychic? Or psycho? Or maybe she just reads the newspaper.*

"Actually, I kind of have to leave in a few minutes."

Rhonda looked horrified. "WHERE ARE YOU GOING?"

"Just to the garage. The band is coming over," I explained. "We need to rehearse." Emphasis on *need*.

Rhonda's eyes bugged out behind her glasses. "BUT THAT'S PERFECT! YOU SHOULD PERFORM!"

I laughed, but Rhonda just kept gazing at me with that happy, hopeful expression.

The band chose that moment to appear.

"Hey, Georgia, what's up?" Nanci's eyes lit up. "Ooh, cookies!" She took three.

"They're homemade," I said, which made Nanci take two more.

"Look what I found!" Patti said, holding up a ceramic calico cat. "Isn't it adorable? I need this. I love animals." She plunked a dollar on the table.

"Are you ready for rehearsal?" Mari asked.

"I WAS JUST TELLING GEORGIA THAT YOU GUYS SHOULD PERFORM RIGHT HERE, RIGHT NOW!" Rhonda screeched. "IT'LL BE LIKE A DRESS REHEARSAL!"

From across the lawn, I heard a noise like an

animal dying, and saw Rafe fall to his knees with his hands over his ears. "DON'T DO IT!" he wailed. "YOU *STINK*!"

Remember a few paragraphs ago? When I thought my brother wasn't so bad? I was over that now.

"Sure, Rhonda," I said. "I think that's a great idea."

Mari shrugged. "Why not?" she said. There were only three other people at the garage sale, anyway: our nosy neighbor Mr. Stanley, ancient Mrs. Bloomgarden, and her Yorkshire terrier, Wilson. They looked like they could stand to rock out.

We set up our stuff in the garage while Rhonda handed out orangeade and acted as the goodwill ambassador for the band. "YOU WON'T BELIEVE HOW AMAZING THEY ARE!" she told Mrs. Bloomgarden.

"She's right—you won't believe it," Rafe agreed.

I strummed a chord. "One-two-three-four!" I shouted, and the band burst into our first song. I have to say that we were getting better. I didn't even get my fingers caught in anything. When we finished the song, there was silence.

Until Rafe hopped up onto a table to do his own performance.

The sad part was that Mrs. Bloomgarden
actually applauded—for Rafe, not us.

That was all the encouragement he needed to
keep going. We Stink was going to have to work
hard to drown out my brother.

"Crank it up," I told my friends. So we did.

The Aftermath

We Stink finished our fifth and final song, and the crowd went wild. And by *wild*, I mean that Mr. Stanley finally took off the earmuffs he had been trying on for the past four songs, and Mrs. Bloomgarden managed to coax Wilson out of the file cabinet, where he had been hiding. She sniffed at me as she carried Wilson away, cooing to him, "Don't worry, poopsie! The big scary noise is all over now."

But at least a couple of people were clapping. "WE STINK RULES!" Rhonda screeched.

Sam stuck his fingers in his mouth and let out a deafening whistle. Yes, that's right—Sam Marks

showed up at my garage sale. I
guess Rhonda must have told him
about it.

I managed to smile at Sam, but I
was feeling kind of seasick. After all,
here I was, playing lousy guitar at a garage sale. So
humiliating.

Clap. Clap. Clap. The sound of sarcastic
applause. I looked around to find out who could be
that rude, but I should have been able to guess.

Missy Trillin, standing by a stack of sweaters. *Gah!
What's* she *doing here?* My stomach shriveled in fear.

"Wow, I really liked your performance, Georgia,"
Missy said with a sneer. "I really liked when it *stopped.*"

"Who's that?" Nanci asked as she snuck another
cookie from the table.

"Nobody," I told her. *Please go away*, I begged
silently. But Missy didn't move, except to pick up
my old Christmas sweater between her thumb and
index finger and grimace at the reindeer on it.

"She seems to think she's somebody." Mari
frowned and folded her arms across her chest as
she watched Missy pick over my family's cast-
off items. I cringed. Missy was acting like she

was searching through a Dumpster in a sketchy neighborhood. All of a sudden, my old, well-loved games, books, and clothes looked like embarrassing trash to me. I wouldn't have been surprised if Missy left and came back wearing a diamond-covered hazmat suit to look through everything else.

Don't look at her, I told myself. Fighting the blush I felt creeping up my neck, I turned to my friends. "Patti, Mari, and Nanci, this is Sam," I said.

My bandmates said hi, and Sam said, "You guys were great."

But Missy couldn't just disappear, of course. She gasped. "Don't tell me you're selling this!" She mockingly held up an old, half-bald troll doll. "And *only* fifty cents?"

I wondered if there was room for me to hide in the file cabinet, now that Wilson had moved on.

"Why is Missy even here?" Sam wanted to know.

"To torture me," I explained.

Rhonda turned her

You're ditching this, Georgia? But you guys have matching fur!

Hands off, Princess! I may look cute, but I've got a wild side.

back on Missy. "ANYONE WANT ORANGEADE?" My bandmates said yes.

"Rhonda's got a lot of…energy," Sam said as we watched her pass around the plate of cookies. She let Nanci take only two.

I wasn't sure what Sam meant by that, so I just said, "She can't help herself." I glanced around the tables, where the items were thinning out. A lot of our stuff had already sold. Grandma Dotty was demonstrating how an exercise bike could also be used as a coatrack. Rafe was trying to convince an older couple that they needed an extra toilet.

"What's up?" Sam asked as I bit my lip. "You look worried."

"It's just—well, I'm a little worried about…Mr. Bananas." I could feel my face redden.

"Stuffed animal?" Sam guessed.

"Yeah. I just don't want him to get sold." I shrugged. "Life isn't the same without a stuffed monkey on your bed, you know?"

Sam smiled. "Yeah."

"Oh, that's *soooo* sweet!" I heard a sugary voice behind me. "Little baby wants her toy monkey back!" Missy rolled her eyes.

I felt my head turn hot down to the tips of my hair. I glanced at Sam. *Does he think I'm an idiot?* I wondered. It was hard to tell. He was too nice to say so.

Missy looked over at the snack table. "Hey, Georgia, why don't you get your *best friend, Rhonda*, to help you look for your dolly?"

"She's not my best friend," I muttered. I knew it

was awful. I glanced over my shoulder and saw that Rhonda was still blissfully handing out orangeade to thirsty bargain hunters. If she'd heard me, she wasn't showing it.

But Missy had heard every word. She smirked.

And suddenly I wished I could smack that smirk right off her face. Who the heck does Missy think she is, anyway? Rhonda's worth ten of her. No, a hundred.

I was starting to accept that I was going to lose my bet with Rafe. I'd never be popular at HVMS, because I'd never be friends with Missy. And that was just fine with me.

CHAPTER 38

Going Bananas

History was made right here at Hills Village Middle School—right in front of my locker!

I got a Boy Gift. That's right: A guy gave me a present.

First.

Time.

Ever!!!!!!!!!!!!!!!!!!!!!!!!!

Hands down, it was the best thing that had happened in the entire pitiful span of my middle school life. I'm bursting with enough happiness that I, Georgia Khatchadorian, could probably spontaneously turn into a cheerleader, right here and now.

The day after the garage sale, I spotted Sam hovering near my homeroom. I waved, and he smiled and said, "I've got something for you." Then he pulled the most awesome present ever out of his backpack.

"Mr. Bananas!" I cried. "You found him!"

Sam grinned and said, "I spotted him as I was leaving. Your grandmother charged me three bucks for him."

"But the tag says a dollar fifty," I noticed.

Sam shrugged. "She could tell I really wanted it, so she jacked up the price."

I hugged my stuffed monkey to my chest. With Mr. Bananas, my room would be mostly back to normal. I had all of the important stuff, anyway. I reached into my backpack. "Let me give you the three dollars."

"Are you kidding? No *way*!" Sam's eyebrows drew together. "I wanted to

Hmph. I'd say I'm worth at least $2.75.

surprise you." He looked down at the floor and said, "I hope you like it."

The walls of my throat swelled—I was so touched, I was practically choking on my own spit. I couldn't talk, so I just smiled and tried to look grateful.

"So...uh...." Sam shuffled his feet and rattled the change in his right-hand pocket.

I managed to find my voice and said, "What is it?" I was sure he was going to say I had something on my face or I smelled weird.

"Well...there's this dance coming up...." Sam looked at me.

"Yes?" My voice was a whisper.

"Um, would you like to—you know—dance? At the dance? Together?"

Somebody pinch me—this must be a dream.

I didn't do anything! I just asked her out!

No, just kidding. Of course, I played it cool.

Let's see, I may have to reorganize my socks or scrub my toilet. But I guess I could reschedule.

"Okay, then," Sam said with a smile after I agreed. "Awesome. Well, see you later."

I stood there for a minute. *Was that real?* I wondered. *Did that just happen?* It seemed highly unlikely, but I was still holding Mr. Bananas. That was evidence. I didn't even care that kids in the hallway were starting to stare at the girl clutching a stuffed monkey. Mr. Bananas could take them any day.

Maybe middle school was starting to look up.

CHAPTER 39

I Find You Offensive,
Mini-Miller the Killer

I gently placed Mr. Bananas in my locker and
floated toward my class. I was wrapped in
a pink, fluffy cloud. Life was a chocolate mountain!
Middle school was a
bucket of sunshine!

Tra-la-la-la-la!

I sense
trouble up
ahead....

"Hey, Limpy." Mini-Miller grunted at me. "My brother has a message for Rafe."

"Is it a fan message?" I asked, feeling my cotton-candy cloud start to melt.

"Nope. It's a warning." Mini-Miller leaned so close to me that I could see his nose hairs. "The message is, 'Watch out, loser. I have friends at Airbrook Arts.'" He gave a snort-laugh.

I think I've already mentioned that nobody is allowed to pick on Rafe but *me*. Especially not after he helped me with the garage sale. And especially *especially* not on the Best Day of My So-Far Middle School Life. "Back off, Mini-Miller," I snarled.

"What did you call me, Knuckle Toes?" Mini-Miller snapped. "What are you gonna do, limp after me?" He gave my shoulder a shove, and I stumbled backward.

Mini-Miller cracked up, and rage took over my body. I swear I'm not responsible for what happened next.

How I Got Back at Mini-Miller in 3 Easy Steps

I froze, watching Mini-Miller hop halfway down
the hallway. My first feeling was horror: *I can't
believe I did that!* My next feeling was excitement: *I
can't believe I did that!*

But I did! I kicked Mini-Miller in the leg!

Mini-Miller was still howling and hopping, so
I stepped around him and started down the hall
feeling more stunned and happy than when I'd won
the regional spelling bee in fifth grade.

Rhonda hooted. She'd seen the whole thing. She
held up her hand for a high five, and I slapped it.
"NOW WHO'S LIMPING, MILLER?" she screeched
as he hobbled away.

That made me smile.

I guess Rhonda and I *are* kind of friends.

Weird friends, but friends.

The Princesses

WHAT DO YOU THINK?" Rhonda squealed the next morning as she thrust a neon-green flyer at me. It was covered in clip art of guitars and sunglasses and music notes and said "WE STINK ROCKS OUT! Come check out the BATTLE OF THE BANDS at the HVMS dance. BE READY FOR AWESOME!"

I could just hear the parts in capital letters screeching at me in Rhonda's voice.

"Um," I said. *What do I think?*

I thought she was nuts.

I thought I didn't want people to watch me humiliate myself.

"The neon green is hurting my eyes" was all I could manage to say.

"YOU DON'T HAVE TO THANK ME!" Rhonda said, crushing me in a hug. "I JUST WANT EVERYONE TO COME SEE HOW GREAT WE ARE!"

"We?" I repeated. I didn't like the sound of that.

"OUI, OUI!" Rhonda pulled out a roll of tape and stuck up one of the flyers. "IT'S SO COOL WHEN YOU SPEAK FRENCH!"

Uh, that wasn't French, Rhonda.

"What's *that*?"

The sharp voice behind me made me jump. When I turned, I saw Missy and her coven of witches. All three of them were scowling at the flyer. They had appeared instantly, like flies attracted to the scent of poo.

Rhonda stood against the wall, as if she had just been caught in a criminal act. I froze too.

We were in for an all-out ballistic attack. *Run, Rhonda! Run!*

But we both just stood there, as if our feet were stapled to the floor.

Missy walked right up to the flyer and ripped it off the wall. Then she gave Rhonda a look that could melt rock. "Why are *you* putting up posters for the dance?"

For a moment, Rhonda was too shocked to speak. Missy had never spoken to her directly before. "BECAUSE MY BAND IS GOING TO BE THERE." Rhonda looked at me for backup.

"*Your* band?" Brittany echoed, gaping at Rhonda. "What instrument do you play—*cow*bell?"

Rhonda blushed. "WELL, I SING, BUT—"

"Please!" Missy cried. "You sing? I can feel my ears bleeding already."

"She's part howler monkey!" Brittany added.

Rhonda hung her head. Now was my chance to tell Missy and the B's exactly what I thought of them.

So, what did I do?

How I Got Back at the Princesses in Three Easy Steps

CHAPTER 41

Georgia's Last Stand

I wanted to help Rhonda...but I also wanted to turn invisible and escape the Wrath of the Princesses. She was trapped in their evil web of insults, and it looked like they were moving in for the kill.

Get away now, I told myself, *while you still can!* I moved, but my feet went the wrong way. Instead of going backward, they went forward. And before I knew what I was doing, I heard myself say, "Shut your lipstick holes! Rhonda's singing with the band, and she rocks!"

The hall went dead silent. Missy's gaze made me feel like a bug that had been pinned to a board with its wings still moving. Everyone was watching us. Rhonda's eyes were so wide that I thought they might fall out of her head and roll around on the floor.

Finally, Missy laughed. Brittany and Bethany laughed too, playing follow the leader, as usual. "Rhonda isn't even your friend," Missy announced. "Remember? You told me so yourself." Then she looked over at Rhonda with a smile, like she'd won.

Rhonda looked at me. "Georgia wouldn't say that," she said, but she didn't sound sure. For the first time ever, she spoke in lowercase letters.

"I—" I tried to speak, but all I could do was make a strangled little squeak.

Rhonda blinked, as if a bug had flown into her face. Her eyebrows pulled together, and then her chin started to quiver. People in the hallway had stopped and were staring. Things were getting quiet, in a bad-quiet kind of way.

Missy let out a loud "Ha!" and walked away, the Princesses trailing after her. I felt the students who lined the hall look away from us. But Rhonda couldn't tear her gaze from mine. I knew what she wanted to hear—that I'd never said that. That it wasn't true.

But I *had* said it.

PS: I just can't draw any of this. It's too hideous. Please, just look away, like everyone else did.

CHAPTER 42

Rhonda Runs

Rhonda stared at me with those huge, damp eyes, and I felt part of myself dissolve like Kool-Aid mix in water. I've always thought that I was a good person. At least, mostly good. But as Rhonda stood there looking at me, TRAITOR written across her face, I started to think I'd never been good at all.

Then she took off like a bullet.

Um, don't you think you're overreacting a little?

I was so surprised that she could move that fast that I didn't even follow her.

Not right away.

By the time I managed to move, Rhonda had blasted through the hallway doors. Then the second bell rang, and I found myself alone in the hall. I was late for class.

I should find her later and apologize, I told myself. But I knew that wasn't good enough. No—I had to find her and apologize *now*. Right away. Even if it meant skipping class and getting in trouble.

Because friendship is more important than French, *oui*?

The first place I looked was the girls' room. No Rhonda. Just a very annoyed eighth grader who I, uh…accidentally barged in on.

Next I tried the cafeteria, but there were just lunch ladies assembling huge trays of goop that looked like reheated goop from yesterday's lunch. Blech.

The only other room in the direction Rhonda had run was the teachers' lounge, and it didn't seem very likely she'd go in there. I knew I didn't want to, since it was a well-known fact that the lounge doubled as Mrs. Stricker's harpy lair.

Rhonda was nowhere to be found.

Who could help me? If I called Mom, she'd just come to school and make a Parental Scene. My bandmates? They don't really *get* Missy Trillin's evil power, or why I don't just throw down with the Princesses. Besides, they were in school too.

In the end, there was only one person I could think of to call.

I'll always owe my brother, because that phone call cleared up everything.

The minute I hung up, I knew what I had to do.

Another Deep Conversation with My Brother

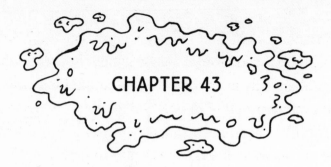

CHAPTER 43

South Nowhere Street

My escape plan was simple yet flawless: I walked out the door. Nobody said anything or tried to stop me.

My heart thrashed like a beached fish, but I didn't look back. I wondered if this was how Rafe felt when he broke a rule at HVMS: excited and a little scared and kind of proud of himself all at the same time.

It hadn't been hard to look up Rhonda's address. Her street was only a few blocks from school. The houses were mostly small and close to the curb, without any front yards at all—just driveways and trash bins. Rhonda's house was as dingy as the rest of them, except her front door looked brand-new, with an oval of stained glass in the center.

As I clanged the huge knocker, I thought I saw the hideous flowered curtains move, just a little. Like someone was peeking out. But no one answered the door. I knocked again. And again.

Rhonda doesn't know who she's dealing with, I thought as I kept knocking. Rafe could've told her—I don't give up that easily.

"GO AWAY!" Rhonda shouted from the other side of the door.

"No!" I knocked again, then rang the doorbell three times in a row just to be annoying.

Rhonda opened the door a crack but left on the security chain, like I was a burglar or a church lady she wanted to avoid. "WE AREN'T EVEN FRIENDS," she announced.

"Don't be dumb. Of course we are."

"WE ARE?" Rhonda looked so hopeful. Her whole face lit up.

"Of *course* you're my friend." I swallowed. "Rhonda...I'm sorry I said that to Missy. The truth is—you're my best friend at HVMS." I knew it was true the minute I said it. Rhonda was sort of weird, and sort of annoying, and—frankly—a style disaster. But she was also unique. And brave. And kind.

I thought about Missy and felt embarrassed. How could I ever have cared what she thought?

Rhonda blinked, and I could see the sparkle of tears on her upper lashes. She pulled off the security chain and opened the door, but she didn't invite me inside. "WHY DID YOU TELL MISSY WE WEREN'T FRIENDS?"

"Because...I'm an idiot," I confessed. "Rhonda, I'm really, really sorry."

186

Rhonda didn't say anything. She just pulled me into a hug.

I'd never been that close to Rhonda before, and I was surprised by her pretty fabric-softener smell and her strong, soft arms. "You're squishing me," I told her.

I can't breathe.

Then we pulled apart, and we both laughed like we were a little embarrassed.

Rhonda swiped at her eyes, and I saw that the tears were gone. "BEST FRIENDS!" she said brightly.

"Okay, but—" I bit my lip. "Rhonda, maybe you could...try not to follow me around so much?"

"SURE, GEORGIA! NO FOLLOWING!" She thought that over for a moment. "BUT WE CAN STILL HANG OUT ALL THE TIME, RIGHT?"

I sighed. I guess it was too much to hope that Rhonda would suddenly turn normal. But that was okay.

Who's normal?

Missy?

Right. I'd take Rhonda any day.

Smacked Down

That evening, I sat perched on my favorite stool at Swifty's as Mom darted back and forth like a dragonfly behind me. The diner was jammed with the usual supper crowd, but the noise didn't bother me. I was reading *The Invention of Hugo Cabret* and drinking a (*gasp!*) chocolate milk shake, which Mom let me have after someone sent it back, insisting that he'd meant to order strawberry. I should have been happy.

But how could I be? Missy and her family were in the corner booth again.

I tried to concentrate on my book, but I couldn't. I kept thinking how much I wanted to grab Missy's glass of water and toss it in her face. She'd probably start melting like the Wicked Witch in *The Wizard of Oz*. And then I'd be all "Clip-clop—I mean, *ding-dong*—the witch is dead!"

Someone kissed my hair, and I looked up to see Mom smiling at me. "How's it going?" She leaned against the stool beside mine. "Good shake?"

"The best."

"Then why are you scowling?"

"I'm not," I lied. "This is just my face."

Mom folded her arms across her chest and glanced over at Missy's table. "How are things going at school?" she asked. When her eyes

THIS IS JUST MY FACE WHEN I'M WITHIN ONE HUNDRED FEET OF MISSY TRILLIN.

met mine, I was suddenly sure Mom knew all about Missy and why I wanted to toss water on her.

"Is this, like, some psychic mom thing?" I asked her.

Mom shrugged. "Do you want to talk about it?"

"Things are…not great," I admitted. "HVMS is like Georgia Smackdown Central."

Mom touched my hair gently. "You've always been good at standing up for yourself with Rafe."

"He's different," I said.

"How?"

"Because he's Rafe!" I stabbed a long spoon into my milk shake and stirred. "He isn't the queen of anything. Missy is."

Mom looked over at Missy's table again. "I know it's hard to stand up for yourself sometimes," she said. "I wasn't any good at it at your age either." She bit her lip. "I still have trouble sometimes."

"I guess it's genetic, then," I said.

Mom frowned for a minute, and she opened her mouth to say something, but Pearl buzzed by with a "Jules, honey, would you be a sweetheart and take care of table eight?"

"Sure," Mom said to Pearl. Then she touched my shoulder. "We'll talk later?"

"Okay," I said, but my words only reached empty air. Mom had darted off again.

I glanced over at Missy and caught her watching me. I narrowed my eyes at her.

Just you wait, Missy Trillin, I thought. *Your queendom is about to get trashed.*

CHAPTER 45

When You Seek Revenge, Dig Two Graves

I'm taking her down, even if I go down with her.

That was the thought that whispered itself over and over in my mind as I lay in bed that night, staring at the ceiling. I wasn't angry. I was perfectly calm. Okay, maybe a little excited.

Missy had insulted, humiliated, and betrayed me. I'd lost my bet with Rafe. I'd gotten detention— twice. There really wasn't anything she could do to me that she hadn't already done.

So I was free.

Free to get revenge.

An image of Mini-Miller flashed in my mind— how he looked as he limped away from me. I solved that problem pretty fast. All it took was a couple of kicks to the shin.

Remembering that made me realize that Mom was right. I *am* good at sticking up for myself. And Missy really isn't any different from Mini-Miller except that her clothes are nicer.

But was kicking her shins the best way to teach Missy a lesson? Probably not.

There were almost too many good alternatives.

CHAPTER 46

Revenge Served Lukewarm

"Georgia, it's seven AM. What on earth are you cooking?" Mom asked when she walked into the kitchen two days later. She blinked blearily at the large pot on the stove.

"Just desserts," I told her. I stirred the thick mass of rice pudding in the pot on the stove.

"Desserts? At seven o'clock on a Thursday morning?"

"I'm bringing the snack today," I said. "Once a week, someone brings in a snack for homeroom." Yes, I felt guilty about lying to my mom. Guilty and a little proud too, because it turned out I was good at it.

"What?" Mom shuffled over to the coffeepot. "Rafe never did that."

"Oh, *Rafe*," I said, shrugging in my most *Rafe-doesn't-ever-participate-in-class-activities* way.

Mom is never really awake before her morning coffee. It isn't hard to fool her.

She just nodded and then suggested that I add a little more nutmeg to the pudding. So I did. Then she offered me a ride to school, since it would be hard to carry the huge plastic tub on the bus.

Perfect!

I got to school early and hid in a stall in the girls' room near the gym. The Princesses occupied it every morning for the ten minutes before homeroom. They needed that time to slather on makeup and figure out ways to insult perfectly nice people, I guess.

"Can you believe what Ashley Parker is wearing today?" I heard Brittany ask as the Princesses waltzed in.

Right on time, I thought gleefully.

"She looks like a cup of cottage cheese," Missy said, and the other Princesses cracked up.

Wait, I told myself. *Wait until the time is right.*

I watched through a crack in the door as Missy smeared on some lip gloss, then pursed her lips in the mirror. "Who's going to tell Madison that she's got broccoli caught in her teeth?" she asked.

"I will," Bethany volunteered. "Who eats broccoli for breakfast, anyway?"

Missy fluffed up her hair. And then she headed into the other bathroom stall.

I counted to five, then climbed up onto the toilet seat, hauled up the tub, and let out a huge "Bluurrggh!"

I fake-barfed warm rice pudding all over Missy. The moment it glopped down the side of her head, she screeched like a cat in heat. Like a cat in heat that's just been puked on *while peeing*.

"BLUURRGGH!!!" I upped the volume of my retching noises.

The other Princesses rushed to help, but the door was locked and Missy was blinded by pudding, so they fumbled around while I just calmly walked out of there as if nothing had happened. My only regret was that I didn't actually get to see Missy, but I had a heck of a great time imagining it.

Mom was right—revenge tastes best when you add a little extra nutmeg.

CHAPTER 47

A Visit with the Lizard King

I was only in homeroom for about five seconds when the school secretary appeared and handed a note to Mr. Grank. When he read it, his head snapped up. "Rafe's SISTER," he announced, "the Lizard King has called you to the Pit of Torment."

"Hmm." I kicked the giant pudding tub behind my desk. "Okay." I followed the school secretary down the hall to the principal's office.

A cricket chirped as I slid into the chair across from the Lizard King, Mr. Dwight. My flesh crawled as his long tongue shot out and his teeth crunched. The room went silent.

Poor cricket.

"I hear you're following in your brother's footsteps, Ms. Khatchadorian," the Lizard King hissed. "Why don't you tell me about this pudding incident?"

"Pudding?" I repeated, as if I had no idea what he was talking about. I was doing my very best *whatever-are-you-talking-about-my-good-sir?* face, with my hands clasped under my chin. It's a proven innocence stance.

Heh-heh-heh. A chuckle from a giant lizard is a scary sound. The Lizard King stretched out a scaly hand and tapped his claws on the arm of his throne. "Come now, Ms. Khatchadorian," he said. "Someone poured a pot of pudding on Missy Trillin, and you are the prime suspect."

MAKING YOURSELF LOOK INNOCENT IN 3 EASY STEPS

How dare you! This is just because I'm Rafe's **sister!**

What kind of diseased—yet brilliant—mind could come up with such a disgusting plan?

Please let me know how I can help you find this evil individual.

Please note: I didn't even lie!

But there was something in the Lizard King's golden gaze that told me he wasn't buying it. I bit my lip and smiled nervously. I wished he would ask me a question or something, just so I wouldn't have to sit there in silence until one of us died.

At that moment, there was a knock at the door. Before the Lizard King could even shout, "Come in," my defense attorney strolled in. Well, I guess he was supposed to be my defense attorney.

It was Rafe.

My client, Georgia, Rafe Khatchadorians sister, is innocent, at least in terms of what she did here, at this school.

At home, well, not so much.

I think I would have preferred Grandma Dotty.

This Deserves Two Chapters

You're pinning this on the wrong girl," my brother said. Rafe plopped a briefcase on the Lizard King's desk, and a pile of papers spilled out. Rafe picked one up. "Exhibit A."

"What's this?" The Lizard King frowned at the paper.

"Her report card from last year." Rafe held out another paper. "Here's the one from the year before that. And the one from the year before. As you can see, the grades are straight A's."

The Lizard King eyed the papers and suddenly let out a stream of fire from his mouth that turned my report cards into ash. But Rafe just went on with his speech.

"Georgia also got 1s in effort, which—honestly—is a little obnoxious. I mean, who tries that hard in study hall?"

"If you're trying to make a point, Mr. Khatchadorian, I suggest you do it soon," the Lizard King told him. "I'm getting hungry."

"Um…right. My point is," Rafe said, "that Georgia was a model student until she came to Hills Village Middle School. And that's my fault."

"Rafe?" I was so surprised, I couldn't think of anything else to say.

My brother turned to face me. "I'm sorry, Georgia," he said. "I know everyone thinks you're guilty because I pulled so many pranks here. But"—he turned back to face the Lizard King—"Georgia is not *me*. Not even close."

There was a long stretch of silence like a curving road leading who knows where. I stared at the Lizard King. He stared back at me. "Do you have anything to add?" Principalzilla asked.

I blinked, and Rafe disappeared.

You knew he was never really there in the first place, right? I mean, why would he be at my school in the middle of the day?

Still…it was a cool thought.

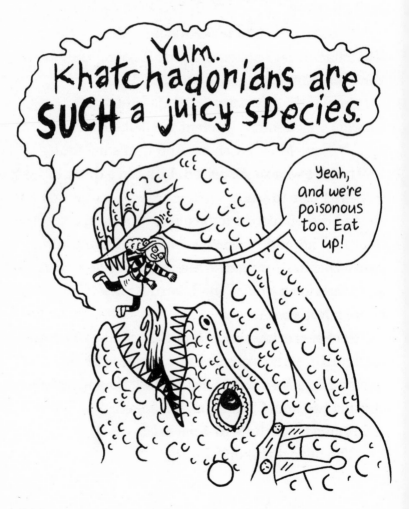

Crime and Punishment

What makes you think I did it?" I asked.

The Lizard King opened a drawer and pulled out a toad. "We have witnesses, Ms. Khatchadorian," he said, popping the toad into his mouth. I could see the bulge in his throat when he swallowed.

"Oh," I said.

I should've known. Bethany and Brittany were in the bathroom too. I guess they had noticed me after all.

"You'll serve a week of detention, of course," the Lizard King said. "And I'm requiring a visit with Ms. Jordan."

"The headshrinker?" I asked.

"The school psychologist, yes." The Lizard King's forked tongue flicked in and out. "She knows your family history."

"Oh, good, maybe she can help me with my genealogy report," I said. (Not really. I said that in my head. Would *you* get sarcastic with a giant lizard?)

The Lizard King leaned forward. His breath smelled like August garbage during a sanitation-worker strike. "The next time you visit my office, Ms. Khatchadorian, I won't hesitate to expel you," he snarled. "I've had it up to the gills with the Khatchadorians."

Well, I've had it up to here with this school, I wanted to shout back. But like I said, you don't mess with a hungry giant lizard.

"You'll be heading to Ms. Jordan now, Ms. Khatchadorian. And remember, next time I won't let you off so easily."

I stood shakily and fled from his lair, glad to be alive. But who knew what awaited me in the next den of despair?

CHAPTER 50

Shrinkology

The minute I sat down in the chair across from hers, the school shrink gave me a warm welcome.

"Please don't say it like that," I told her.

Ms. Jordan leaned back in her chair and studied me. "Don't say it like what?" she asked.

"With all capital letters and an exclamation mark at the end." I sat on my hands. "Rafe and I aren't the same person. And besides, he's not as bad as everyone around here thinks."

I thought about how he'd helped out at the garage sale and defended me to the Lizard King— even though that hadn't really happened—and I got a warm, fuzzy feeling.

"Hmm." Ms. Jordan picked up a pencil and bounced it off the table a few times. "So—what brings you here, Georgia?"

Um, royal command of the Lizard King?

"It's a long story."

"I have a lot of time on my hands," Ms. Jordan said.

I sighed. Clearly, I wasn't going to escape until I'd delivered my autobiography.

I tried to give her the condensed version.

MY EXTRAORDINARY FIRST ELEVEN YEARS

1. I was born with lopsided hips.

2. I was relentlessly tortured by my brother from the earliest years.

3. Because of my suffering, I became a great defender of the helpless and less fortunate.

4. I cultivated my powers of persuasion and raised my voice for the needy.

5. Despite the constant distraction and abuse by my brother, I achieved academic excellence.

"I'm wondering if you can speed this story up a bit," Ms. Jordan said.

"I spilled pudding on Missy Trillin's head while she was taking a pee."

"I see." Ms. Jordan nodded. "Now I think we're getting somewhere."

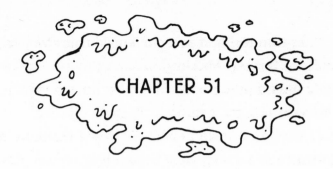

CHAPTER 51

More Shrinkology

It was **SO AWESOME** I almost morphed into a cheerleader— again!

So, you spilled pudding on Missy's head," Ms. Jordan said. She poked her flabby cheek with the eraser end of her pencil. "How did that make you feel?"

"Horrible," I said.

Ms. Jordan lifted her eyebrows.

"It was actually kind of great," I admitted.

"I assume you had reasons for pouring pudding on Missy Trillin," Ms. Jordan said. She tucked the pencil behind her ear.

"Good reasons," I replied. "Missy's a bully."

Ms. Jordan pursed her lips as if she doubted my statement. "I've seen your permanent record. You're a good student, Georgia. Or you were. Until you came to HVMS."

I shrug.

"Are you at all worried about how your mother will react when she hears what happened?"

I flushed red and hot, like a giant pimple. I meant to say "no way," but it came out in a whisper as "yes."

"Hmm." Ms. Jordan pulled the pencil out from behind her ear and scratched her scalp with it. "But your brother, Rafe, breaks rules all the time, doesn't he?"

"So?"

The edge of her lip curled up. "So your mother should be used to it by now."

"I told you, I'm not Rafe."

"Mmm." The school shrink leaned forward and stared at me like I was a frog she wanted to dissect. "Do you think, Georgia, that your physical deformity fuels your need to act out?"

I felt like I'd just been punched in the face.
I couldn't think of anything to say…and then I
thought of a *lot* of things to say. It involved a lot of
words that would have to be bleeped out if I were
telling this story on TV.

But I didn't say anything. I just sat there,
breathing deeply.

"I see I've struck a nerve," Ms. Jordan said.

"I'm going to class now," I announced. Then I
stood up and walked out of her office, leaving the
rest of the shrunken heads behind me.

CHAPTER 52

Jeanne Galletta Is Actually a Princess

After school, I headed back to the cafeteria to help Mr. Adell wipe down filthy tables. The bacteria bucket didn't seem as gross the second time around. I guess my standards had gone way down.

At least this time there were no Princesses watching my every move. Or so I thought.

"Georgia?" Jeanne tapped on the glass door.

I ignored her. Which wasn't easy, by the way.

I yanked the door open. "What do you want?" I didn't sound too friendly, I guess, but I didn't care. I scanned her hands to make sure she wasn't holding any revenge pudding.

"I, uh, I wanted to let you know that Missy, Bethany, and Brittany don't want your band to play at the dance—"

"Whatever," I said, but Jeanne kept talking.

"—but I told them to get lost."

"You—what?" I was so surprised that I dropped my smelly sponge.

Jeanne looked over her shoulder, as if she were afraid someone might be spying on us. "I know Missy has…uh…personal reasons for not wanting you to perform. But she needs to get over it."

"Yeah," I said. I was a little unsure how to respond. Jeanne was doing me a favor, but it was a favor that I wasn't sure I wanted. Still, it was nice of her. "Um, thanks?"

Jeanne nodded and turned away. She started for the door, then stopped and turned back. "Georgia, the other day, when I told you I liked your hair?"

"Yeah?" I narrowed my eyes.

"I just wanted you to know that I was serious,"

she said. "I can't stand Missy," Jeanne added. "I wish I'd had the guts to pour pudding on her head." Then Jeanne pushed open the door and walked out.

I stood there for a moment, watching her walk away. My opinion of Rafe had just shot up about ten

miles. Of course, it started out about fifteen miles below the surface of the earth, but still…maybe his taste in friends wasn't so bad after all.

Maybe he was the only person who knew a real princess when he saw one.

CHAPTER 53

Practice Doesn't Always Make Perfect

After detention, I hurried home for rehearsal. The dance was *tomorrow night*, so it was pretty much our last chance to really rock out before the Battle of the Bands. We even had an audience— Rafe, Rhonda, and Mom.

Hold it. She's SMOKIN'!

"Wow," Rafe said after about a half hour. "That was amazing."

"Really?" Patti asked.

"Yeah—" My brother's eyes were wide, like he was dead serious. "You guys sounded exactly like a tractor falling off a cliff."

"DON'T LISTEN TO HIM!" Rhonda said. "YOU GUYS SOUNDED GREAT!"

I glanced at my mom. "Yes," she said slowly. "I think you girls are...improving."

I groaned. *That was the best she could come up with*, I thought. *And she's my* mom! *We must be really bad.*

We Stink was going to sink like the *Titanic*.

Mari sighed. "Well, we'll just have to get up there and do our best," she said.

"I'm not worried," Nanci said. She pulled a bag of chips out of her backpack and ripped it open. "It's our first gig—it's okay if we aren't perfect."

"It's okay for you guys," I grumbled. "It isn't your school. Even if you embarrass yourselves, it won't be in front of anyone you know."

"WHAT'S EMBARRASSING ABOUT BEING AWESOME?" Rhonda wanted to know.

Nanci looked thoughtful as she crunched a chip.

"Do you want to back out?" Patti asked.

Yes, I thought. But then Missy's evil, grinning face swam into my mind, and I realized that was exactly what she wanted. I'd rather do all Rafe's chores for six months (which I was going to have to do anyway) than do something to make Missy happy. Besides, I couldn't let Jeanne down after she'd stood up for us. "No," I said at last.

Mari smiled. "It's going to be fine."

"Yeah," Rafe agreed. "Like a *two-hundred-dollar* fine! For a noise violation." He cracked up at his own joke.

"Oh, be quiet, Rafe," I told him. I gritted my teeth and looked down at my guitar. *Don't worry*, I said to myself. *You won't be that bad.*

And even if you are, it doesn't matter. Things can't get any worse at school than they are now, right?

Right?

CHAPTER 54

How I Became a Princess

I swear I was about to tell Mom about the pudding and the detention and all of that the minute my bandmates headed home. Really. It's just...I was a little worried that she wouldn't let me go to the dance if I mentioned it. I wanted to make sure I said it the right way....

3 STRATEGTES for CONFESSING to MOMS by G.K.

Option 1: Confuse her.

Mom, I have some sort of, kind of not terrible but not great bad news that's not even half as bad as the news that Rafe brings home all the time yada yada yada...

Option 2: Inspire pity.

Dearest mother, I have been betrayed by the very classmates I had so hoped would accept me for who I am.

Option 3: Blame someone else.

This is **his** fault!

"I CAN'T WAIT TO SHOW YOU MY DRESS FOR THE DANCE!" Rhonda said. She'd followed me home from school again to watch us practice, but somehow I didn't mind so much. "WHAT ARE YOU WEARING, GEORGIA?"

VERY COUTURE! I LOVE IT!

Mom cocked her head, as if she was interested in hearing the answer.

"I...I haven't thought about it," I confessed.

"WELL, THINK ABOUT IT!" Rhonda cried. "YOU'LL BE UP ONSTAGE!"

"And it's your first school dance," Mom agreed. "Rhonda's right. I'm taking you to Smythe and Smythe."

"The fancy department store?" I asked. I'd actually set foot in there only once before. A very tall, very scary-looking woman with no eyebrows squirted me with a bottle of stinky perfume. It took two days to get the smell off.

So that's how I forgot to mention my detention

and instead ended up going shopping with Rhonda and my mom.

I headed straight for the sale rack, where fashions come to die of humiliation.

The potato-sack fad never caught on.

I would never survive Rafe's few choice words about this. one.

Great for supermodels... or giraffes!

"None of these really seem like me," I said.

"WHAT ABOUT THIS ONE?" Rhonda asked.

From Rhonda's excited tone, I could only imagine what she had just picked up.

IT'S SO US!

Fortunately, my imagination was way off.

"Oh, I love it!" Mom said, taking the hanger from Rhonda and grabbing my arm. "Georgia, you have to try it on."

So I did.

I knew it was the perfect dress even before I stepped out of the dressing room. But when I came out, Rhonda let out a screech and tackled my mom in a huge hug. Mom said, "You look beautiful, Georgia."

I turned and gazed at myself in the three-way mirror. Beautiful? Well, she's my mom. But I definitely looked pretty good.

"IN YOUR FACE, MISSY TRILLIN!" Rhonda squealed.

I smiled. *Yeah*, I thought. *I look kinda princessy. In a good way.*

This could really work.

HVMS

MISSY TRILLIN'S TIPS FOR CLONES

FASHION MAGAZINE

HOW GEORGIA GOT THAT LOOK!

FROM LAME TO FAME: LATEST VILLAGE "IT" GIRL TELLS HER INSPIRING TRUE STORY

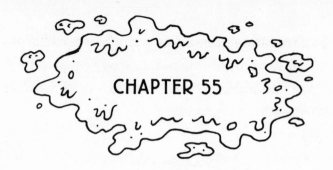

CHAPTER 55

The Strange Truth

I was still wondering how to bring up the detention thing when Mom and I got home from shopping. But Mom made a beeline for her room and started digging around in the bottom of her closet. "What are you doing?" I asked.

"You'll see." Mom grunted. Then she pulled out a battered old shoe box. She flashed me a triumphant grin and said, "Come sit by me."

It was actually kind of cozy there in my mom's closet. She lifted the lid of the box. Inside was a pile of old photos.

"Um, you can burn this one," I said, picking up

a picture of me dressed as a chicken for Halloween when I was three.

"Are you kidding?" Mom chuckled. "That's adorable!"

Grandma Dotty's doing

Before he got so annoying

"Here it is!" Mom held out a photo.

"Who's that?" I asked.

"It's me!" Mom actually laughed. "At the sixth-grade dance."

"You?" I stared at the photo. "Wow. It's kinda weird how I really don't look anything like you did in sixth grade."

Grandma Dotty appeared in the doorway. "Why would you two look alike?" she asked.

"Mother, do you mind?" My mom pushed the closet door shut. For a minute it was dark, and I couldn't see anything. Then Mom reached up and pulled the light chain. Maybe it was the overhead lighting, but my mother's face looked weird.

I should've brought up the detention right then. Instead, I whispered, "What's up with Grandma?"

"What do you mean?

"I mean, you're my mom, but Grandma Dotty doesn't seem to think we should act alike or look alike. Is she...okay?" I was starting to worry about Grandma's mind. It was like her brain was taking longer and longer vacations from her body. I didn't blame it—I wouldn't want to be stuck in her head all the time either.

"Tell her, Jules," Grandma said from behind the closet door. "She's smart—she'll figure it out. Tell her, or I will."

"Mother, would you just—leave! Please!"

Mom had never yelled at Grandma before—not in front of me. This was getting seriously weird. But I heard Grandma Dotty's footsteps leaving the room, and then Mom sighed.

"Georgia, I've got something I need to tell you," she said, looking down at the funky sixth-grade photo of herself. "But I don't know how to say it." She sounded so freaked out that I thought she was getting ready to tell me all about the birds and the bees. To which I can only say:

YUCK.

"Um—don't worry, Mom. I learned all about that stuff in health class last year," I said.

Mom chewed her lip. "No, Georgia…" She took my hand and pressed my fingers really gently. "Sweetheart, I don't know how to say this, so I'm just going to say it…."

Sorry. That transcript may not be entirely right. My brain sort of short-circuited after the word "adopted."

But it made sense. It explained everything. Why I didn't look like Mom. Why I didn't act like Rafe.

Grandma Dotty's brain wasn't being eaten by worms.

My *life* was.

CHAPTER 56

Jules Explains It All

When Rafe and Leo were born, I was so happy. But Leo got sick. And then he died," Mom went on.

"It's still really, really hard for me to talk about. I didn't want to leave the house—ever. I didn't want Rafe to leave the house. I wouldn't let him play with anything hard, or touch anything that had been on the floor, or even sit on the couch, because he might fall off. I was going crazy, and I was making us both miserable. And that was when I realized that I needed more to think about, not less. I needed another outlet. I had all this extra love to give, and you needed someone to love you. So I adopted you."

Mom stopped. She stared at me like she was trying to read my mind. I could tell she really wanted me to understand....

But I wasn't sure that I *did* understand.

"You adopted me to replace Leo?"

"No," Mom said, but her strange, shaky voice made it sound like "maybe" to me.

Rafe and Leo were twins. I could never take Leo's place. No wonder I always felt like I had to be perfect—like I wasn't quite how I was supposed to be. I *wasn't*.

Because I wasn't Leo. And I never could be.

CHAPTER 57

I'm Not Going

I didn't tell my mom about the detention. What would have been the point? Clearly, I wasn't going to the dance.

I went to my room and climbed through my window, onto the roof of the back porch. That's where I go when I want to be alone.

I looked up at the sky. The moon was lopsided—almost round, but not quite. There are too many lights where I live, so I could see only one or two stars.

"Are you going to make a wish on one?" Rafe asked. He was leaning halfway out his window.

I thought of all my usual wishes, like winning

the lottery, becoming a famous Disney Channel star, rocking out at the Battle of the Bands....

None of those wishes seemed to matter anymore. "What's the point of wishing?" I asked.

Rafe shrugged. "Maybe it'll come true. Do you mind if I sit out here with you?" "Yes," I told him.

"Great," Rafe said, and climbed out his window to join me.

I sighed. Actually, I had meant *yes, I do mind*, not *yes, come sit with me*. But Rafe was being nice, and I didn't really have the energy to tell him I wanted to be alone.

Rafe didn't say anything. He just lay beside me, looking up at the lumpy moon.

"Did you know?" I asked into the night air.

There was silence from him for a long time. Out in the yard, a lonely cricket chirped. I was starting to think maybe Rafe had fallen asleep or something, and I was about to poke him, when he said, "Yes."

"When did Mom tell you?"

"She didn't have to. I remember."

I knew we weren't going to get along from day one.

I felt dizzy. I was glad I was lying down.

"That's why Mom always gives you all the attention—that and your leg."

"All the attention?" I repeated. "Are you serious?"

"If I didn't act crazy, Mom wouldn't even remember I was around," Rafe said. "It's been that way since the day we brought you home."

The day we brought you home. There was something about those words that made me start to cry. I tried to do it as quietly as possible. Tears leaked out the sides of my eyes and trickled into my hair.

"You're my sister, Georgia," Rafe said. "You always have been." And then he took my hand, and I thought I might just break into jagged little pieces.

I blinked back my tears and swallowed hard. "So, like, are we supposed to hug now?" I asked Rafe.

"No, thanks," he said. "Your breath is as bad as your band."

"I knew you were in there," I said.

"What?"

"Never mind."

"So, isn't your dance tonight? Why aren't you

getting dressed?" Rafe rolled over onto his side so he could look at me.

"I'm not in the mood," I told him.

"You're going to bail on the band?" Rafe sounded shocked.

I hadn't thought of that at all. Rafe was right—I couldn't just let down Mari, Nanci, and Patti. And Sam. I'd promised to dance with him. If I didn't show, he'd have spent three dollars on Mr. Bananas for nothing.

I rolled over so that I was facing my brother. "You're right," I told him.

My brother grinned at me. "As usual," he said.

"This is a deep moment, Rafe—don't ruin it."

"Sorry."

I'm taking Rafe's advice? Isn't that one of the signs of the apocalypse?

CHAPTER 58

My First Middle-School Dance
(Will I Ever Forget This Moment?)
(I Have No Idea.)
(Meh—I'll Probably Forget It.)

I stood in front of the double doors, breathing deeply. I could hear music coming from the dance on the other side of the wall. *You can do this*, I told myself. *Just walk in.*

But I couldn't make my feet move. Missy had gotten into my head, like a fly that just keeps buzzing around and around until it drives you crazy. I could already hear all the nasty things she would say: "Get out of here, LIMPY! Just DRAG yourself right back out the door. Your dress is totally LAME."

There was only one thing to do.

I pushed open the doors and gasped. The gym looked incredible. The dance committee had done something amazing with silver balloons and silver netting that hung down from the ceiling. And I have no idea how they got the place to stop stinking of sneaker fungus, but the entire gym smelled like Missy's shampoo.

SMACK!

You bent my crown!

In one corner, there was a table loaded with cupcakes and cookies. And at the far end of the gym was a stage with a red curtain. Glittery silver letters spelled out BATTLE OF THE BANDS!

My stomach flipped like an Olympic gymnast. I couldn't believe Missy had managed to pull off a theme like "Moonlight in Venice" in the gym.

"Hey!" Sam tapped me on the shoulder. "You look great. I really like your dress." He gave me a huge, dimply smile.

My flipping stomach returned. It was really going for a gold medal.

"Thanks!" I said. He was looking cute too, but I didn't know how to say so without sounding dorky. So I ended up with, "I like your tie."

"I knew you'd like it," he said. It had monkeys on it.

I blushed. *He picked out that tie for me!* My stomach tried to kick its way past my rib cage. I wanted to think of something to say, but I guess my brain was on a break. So I stood there awkwardly for a moment, watching my classmates on the dance floor. The disco ball sent doughnuts of light spinning around the room. It was kind of like being in a snow globe.

"Do you want to dance?" Sam asked.

"Of course she doesn't." The voice came from behind Sam. "Do you think she wants to limp all over the floor?" Missy stood there in her sparkly princess dress, with her glossy hair and Ultrabrite teeth, sneering at me.

My stomach finally stumbled, then fell with a *splat*. I wanted to say something, but I was too stunned.

"Missy, why don't you go take a flying leap off a gondola?" Sam said, taking my hand. He led me toward the dance floor, but I hesitated at the edge.

"What's wrong?" Sam asked.

I bit my lip. "Sam—Missy is…"

"A moron?" Sam guessed.

"Well…but maybe she's right." I glanced down at my feet. My skin felt cold and clammy, as if my embarrassment had just lowered the temperature in the room. I felt a little sick and wondered if maybe I was coming down with something.

Sam touched my shoulder gently. "You don't have to dance if you don't want to, Georgia," he said.

His eyes were so blue. They reminded me of these pretty glass mineral-water bottles that Grandma Dotty likes to buy at garage sales. I imagined light shining through his eyes, the way they shine through the bottles when Grandma puts them on the windowsill. Suddenly, the cold that had settled over me dropped away.

It felt good to know that Sam would understand if I didn't want to embarrass myself out on the dance floor. But there was only one problem....

"I *do* want to dance," I said. I really, really did.

I mean, this was my moment!

I was at my first middle-school dance!

A sweet, cute boy wanted to dance with me!

It's not like this was happening every weekend.

Sam smiled. "Good. Because you already promised you would dance with me."

We stepped out onto the floor just as the music stopped. A slow song started.

Sam put his arms at my waist, and I thought for sure that I might faint. Instead, I rested my head on his shoulder. Dancing wasn't hard at all—I just shuffled back and forth. Maybe it was just the scent of Missy's shampoo mixed with the disco ball lighting that affected my brain, but I felt like I was in a happy, beautiful dream.

I never wanted it to end.

But, of course, three minutes later it did.

CHAPTER 59

Band Gone Weird

Don't make me go," I begged Sam. I just wanted to stay on the dance floor, shuffling around with him forever.

"I can't wait for you guys to perform," Sam said. "It'll be great!"

"Great?" I repeated. "Yeah, great for *Missy*."

"You aren't worried about her, are you?" Sam asked. "What could she possibly do to you?"

Oh, probably nothing too serious. Force all the other kids to boo us? Bombard my head with tomatoes? Send Fabio to pee on my leg?

Sam must have seen the horror on my face, because he said, "It'll be fine. I promise."

"Just don't let her use a hook on me."

"You mean like Captain Hook?"

That was a *really* scary thought. "*Any* kind of hook."

Sam promised and then walked me over to the stage. Nanci, Mari, and Patti were there, listening as the first band—or should I say *bland*—lulled everyone to sleep.

Rhonda rushed up to us. "LET'S BUST SOME EARDRUMS!" she Rhonda-whispered.

"Um, guys, I told Rhonda she could sing a song with us," I said. Then I kind of scrunched up my face. I'm not sure what I was expecting. Gasps of horror? Shouting?

"Okay," Nanci said.

Mari nodded. "Sounds good."

"Welcome to We Stink," Patti told Rhonda, who lit up like a Christmas tree.

"Well, okay, then," I said. *I mean, why shouldn't Rhonda perform with us? It's not like we can be much worse than we are.*

The band before ours finished up, and Missy announced us. "Okay, everyone. I've heard this next band, and let me say this: It really lives up to its name. So put in your earplugs—and maybe put on a blindfold too. Let's hear it for They Stink!"

A few halfhearted claps. Someone whistled. Probably Sam.

But Rhonda just stomped right up to the microphone. "ARE YOU READY TO ROCK?"

"Yeah!" Sam shouted. His voice echoed through the silent gym.

"I CAN'T HEAR YOU, HVMS! I SAID—ARE YOU READY TO ROCK?!"

"Yeah!" A few more people chimed in this time.

"LET'S SHAKE THIS HOUSE!" Rhonda turned to us. "ONE, TWO, ONE-TWO-THREE-FOUR!"

We let it rip. Rhonda grabbed the microphone and shredded it!

Let me say this: Rhonda was AMAZING.

Yes, I'm serious.

No, really.

Really!

We Stink sounded awesome! All that time struggling with our instruments had finally paid off. My fingers found the chords, and I didn't even drop my pick.

Nanci was drumming instead of eating pie. Mari's bass had all of the strings, and Patti had even remembered to plug in her keyboard.

And Rhonda's crazy, screechy voice actually sounded perfect with our crazy, screechy instruments. We were a slamming heavy-metal band!

The crowd danced madly, punching their fists in the air. But I really knew we were good the minute I glanced over at Missy. She looked like she was about to throttle someone.

I grinned.

And the band played on.

CHAPTER 60

Princess Gone Wild

When we finished, the crowd went wild. People were screaming. I felt their voices vibrate through my chest.

I had been so worried that I would embarrass myself that I had never even thought about how good it might feel to be onstage. But the crowd's approval roared up to me, and I felt like a volcano, ready to explode with happiness.

HVMS kept shouting. Someone threw a pair of boxer shorts onstage.

I don't want to know where those came from.

Rhonda beamed at me. "I TOLD YOU WE WOULD ROCK!"

The crowd was chanting, "MORE! MORE! MORE!"

This is usually the place where I would say something like *And then I woke up*.

But this was real.

"Let's do another one!" I shouted over the noise of the crowd. But Missy Trillin was already storming onto the stage. She grabbed the microphone and yanked it out of Rhonda's hands. Then she hit the crowd with her Death Glare.

The room was as silent as a grave. My grave.

"Well," Missy said finally. The microphone made her voice boom off the walls. "That was surprising. Especially since everyone knows Georgia's so... *lame*." She smirked.

For a moment, nobody spoke. My throat burned like I'd swallowed some hot lava. Everything got blurry. *Run!* my brain shouted. *Don't let her get the hook!*

But before I could turn and rush away, someone shouted, "Boo!" Then someone else joined in. "Boo, Missy!"

I heard Sam's voice. "We want an encore!"

"En-core! En-core! En-core!" the crowd chanted. I couldn't believe it. They were standing up to Missy. Was her power starting to crumble?

"I'm sorry, we don't have time," Missy said into the microphone. "The next band is—"

"En-CORE! En-CORE!"

The shouts washed down on me like cold rain. I blinked, and my tears cleared away. I watched Missy speaking into the microphone, but I couldn't hear what she was saying. The crowd was too loud. They wanted another song.

And—right at that moment—I realized something important: I wanted to give them one.

"Be quiet!" Missy hollered, but nobody heard her. Or maybe they did, but they just didn't care.

"Get off the stage, Missy," I snapped, reaching for the microphone.

Missy stuck out her foot and I stumbled forward, windmilling my arms. I tried to regain my balance, and I reached out—

A couple of kids in the front row caught me. I wasn't hurt. I looked up just in time to see Missy gaping down at her missing skirt in horror. Then she stared out at everyone—laughing at her.

Rhonda offered Missy a tambourine to hold in front of her underpants, but Missy just batted it away. Then she let out a shriek and ran off the stage.

Rhonda looked down at me. "SHOULD WE DO ANOTHER SONG?" she asked.

"Definitely!"

Rhonda held out a hand and hauled me up onstage. I strapped on my electric guitar as the crowd let out a huge cheer. We tore up the next song, and two more after that. Then we had to bow for, like, five full minutes. Rhonda was eating it up—blowing kisses to the crowd and winking at the cutest boys.

As we headed offstage, I gave Rhonda a high five. Nanci, Mari, and Patti were squealing with excitement.

"I can't wait for us to play at Airbrook Arts!" Mari said.

Oh, boy. I wasn't sure what Rafe would think of that. He'd probably spend the whole performance in the bathroom, barfing, with his hands over his ears.

"WE WERE GREAT! RIGHT, GEORGIA?" Rhonda asked.

"You were fantastic, Rhonda," I told her. Then I gave her a hug as she blushed and smiled.

"Georgia?" asked a soft voice behind me. I don't know how I heard it over the cheers of the crowd, but I did.

"Um, Georgia, I just wanted to say that I thought you were really good. I'm sorry Missy was so mean out there."

"Thanks, Bethany," I said.

"I'm Brittany."

"Oh. Okay. Well, anyway, thanks."

"She's really awful, isn't she?" Brittany asked. She looked like she was about to cry.

I felt sort of bad. It must have been hard to have Missy as a friend. I squeezed her shoulder. "Yeah, she's horrible."

Brittany burst into tears.

Just then Sam shouted, "Georgia!" I saw him waving, hurrying over to join me. My performance was over. My band had rocked. The best part? Now I could spend the rest of the evening dancing with Sam.

I grinned and waved back.

Best.

Dance.

Ever!

We'll turn back into princesses at midnight, right, Missy?

I look horrible in orange!

Be quiet, or I'll carve you two into jack-o'-lanterns!

CHAPTER 61

My Mom Is...My Mom

How was it?" Mom asked when I climbed into the car later that night.

My mind was whirling with all the things I wanted to tell her about.

"We won the Battle of the Bands!" I said. "And I danced with Sam! It was, like, the best night of my life!"

"I'm so glad! You and your band worked very hard." Mom smiled warmly. "You deserved it, Georgia."

Suddenly, I felt like a heel. Mom had bought me this great dress and encouraged me to perform... and I hadn't even told her the truth about my detention. If I'd told her, she probably would've grounded me, and the best night of my life never would've happened....

I felt ill, like I'd accidentally stolen something. Mom deserved to know the truth.

I took a deep breath. "Mom, I poured pudding on Missy Trillin's head and I got a week of detention plus I had to talk to the school psychologist but I swear that's it and I'll never do anything bad again and I'm reallyreallyreallyreally sorry."

"Oh, Georgia," Mom said. She shook her head.

"I know."

"I wish you had told me."

"I know. I meant to tell you before the dance, but—"

"No, Georgia," Mom shook her head and reached for my hand. "I wish you had told me you were having so much trouble with Missy. I could've helped you."

I sighed. "I kind of think it's solved now."

"That's good. And Georgia—about being adopted. I'm sorry. I should've told you earlier. I guess…I guess I hoped it wouldn't matter."

We sat there in the dark parking lot for a while. Did being adopted matter? In some ways, it did. Somewhere out in the world, I had a biological mother and father. We shared genes. That was important.

But right here, in this dark car, I had a mother who'd raised me.

We shared love. And, honestly, that's the most important thing of all.

"I'm sorry I've been kind of a lousy daughter lately," I said after a moment.

Mom turned in her seat to look me in the face. "Georgia," she said, "I wish you hadn't gotten into trouble at school. But you're not a lousy daughter. You're wonderful. And even if you were lousy—I'd still love you." She reached out and pulled me close. She smelled of apple pie from the diner, and coffee, and a million other things that made her smell like Mom. "We're a family, Georgia. Family is forever."

We hugged for a long time. After a while, Mom let out a little squeak. Her body shook.

"What?" I asked, pulling away.

Mom squeaked again, and I realized she was laughing. "Pudding," she said.

That made me chuckle too. "Yeah."

"You really *are* Rafe's sister, aren't you?" Mom's eyes sparkled, and I could tell that—in a weird way— she was proud of us.

Am I like Rafe? I thought about my last few weeks at HVMS. They certainly were filled with...mayhem.

"Yeah," I said at last. "I guess I am."

One Other Thing

Since it was True Confessions time, I told Mom about my grades.

"My teachers won't give me a chance," I said.

"I'll take care of it," Mom said, and I knew she would. When Mom went in to talk to teachers, she was like a lioness protecting her cubs. I almost felt bad for the Lizard King and Mr. Grank.

Almost.

"You should have told me about this earlier too," Mom said.

"I thought you'd be disappointed," I admitted.

"Georgia, I care about your grades, but only because I know you like school." Mom started the car and backed out of our parking spot. "You're good at it. You like to work hard, and you enjoy getting the grades you deserve. And I'm going to do everything I can to make sure your teachers understand that you aren't Rafe."

I'm not Rafe, my drowsy mind whispered. An image of myself onstage, with Rhonda, floated through my head. I saw Missy's surprised face when I yanked off her skirt, Brittany's tears as she realized how awful her friend was, and Sam's sweet, dimpled smile as he asked me to dance. I remembered Mini-Miller's shock as I kicked him in the shin. I saw Jeanne's expression when she told me she really did like my green hair. *I'm not Rafe*, I thought. *I'm Georgia. I'm me.*

And for the first time in weeks, I was positive that middle school was going to be okay.

It's really not hard to tell us apart. I'm the cute one. And the smart one.

And the one with the big mouth.

True.

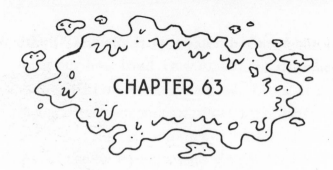

CHAPTER 63

Cease-Fire Between Rafe and Me (This Is Real. Honest.)

I was just about to fall asleep when someone knocked on my door.

"It's Rafe—can I come in?"

I was immediately suspicious. Usually, Rafe doesn't knock—he just barges right in.

"Okay," I said, sitting up in bed.

"How did the band do?" He sat down on the edge of my bed.

"Rhonda sang. It was amazing," I told him.

"I knew you guys would be good."

"What?" I kicked him a little with my blanketed foot. "You think we stink!"

Rafe shrugged. "You don't really stink that bad," he admitted.

I've smelled worse.

Sniff. Sniff.

We haven't.

"I'm glad you made me go to the dance," I said.

Rafe shrugged. "I didn't *make* you."

"Still. I wouldn't have gone if it weren't for you. So..." I bit my lip. "Thanks." Wow. I just said "thank you" to my brother. This night was definitely one for the record books.

Rafe looked down at my old quilt. He traced the pattern with his finger. "Listen, uh...maybe a brother and sister shouldn't fight so much."

"Are you talking about a specific brother and sister?" I asked.

Rafe rolled his eyes and then looked into my face. "Me and you," he said.

"Well, it's not my fault, Rafe."

"I know."

"Oh," I said. "So—are you saying it's your fault?"

"I'm saying we could both do a better job. I mean, what are we fighting about, anyway? It's almost like it's just a habit. It's not like we hate each other. Right?"

Then I waited for him to say something sarcastic. I waited quite a while. "You have a point," I said at last. "Maybe we even like each other," I went on bravely. "I mean, sometimes."

"Yeah." Rafe nodded. "Good." Then he stood up and walked out of my room.

Wow. That was unexpected.

I guess I'd finally worn him down, like a bar of soap.

Just don't use me to wash your armpit.

Cease-Fire Over, War Resumes

Well, it was nice while it lasted.

"Rafe!" I screeched as I dug a spoon into my muesli the next morning. "There's a snail in my cereal!"

"I thought you liked escargot," Rafe shot back. "It's French."

Oooooh, I'm going to GET him for this! I thought, and the thought actually made me kind of…happy.

It had only been a few hours, but I'd missed the sneak attacks. The tactics. The squealing. The repartee. (Look it up. Merriam-Webster has an online dictionary.)

Hey, it's nice when Rafe is being sweet. But it's more *fun* when he's being Rafe.

CHAPTER 65

And...I Lost the Bet

Surprised?

I wasn't.

I didn't get straight A's—I got a B+ in English—and the Princesses did NOT get personality transplants and suddenly become my friends.

Georgia, you are so cool.

We love you now.

Uh, no, thanks.

Let's do each other's nails.

Woof?

Then again, Rafe didn't win the bet either.

I DO have friends, and I'm NOT begging to leave HVMS. So I guess it's what you call a draw.

Speaking of drawing, I showed my artwork to Rafe, and he helped a little.

This much:

So I guess it isn't so bad being Rafe Khatchadorian's SISTER.

It's much worse.

(Gotcha, Rafe! It's so *easy*.)

**LET'S GET ONE
THING STRAIGHT:
RAFE KHATCHADORIAN
IS NO BOOGER-EATER!**

**HE'S JUST STUCK
AT SUMMER CAMP
WITH ONE.**

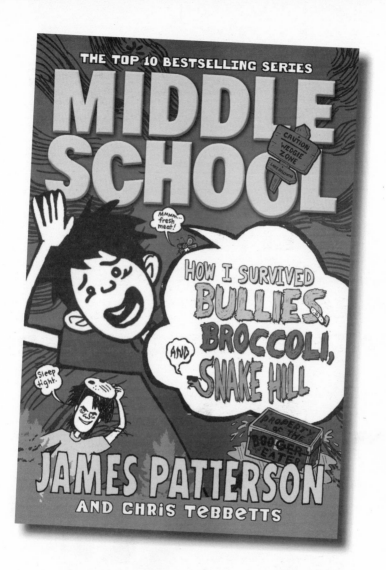

**TURN THE PAGE FOR
A SNEAK PREVIEW!**

CHAPTER 1

A SLAM-BAM ENDING(?) FOR OUR STORY

Let's get one thing out of the way here.

My name is Rafe Khatchadorian, and if you already know me, then you know that trouble tends to follow me around like a bad smell. But if we've never met before, I just want to say—it's not my fault! (Okay, not always.) I hope you can trust me for a little while and give me a chance to explain.

In fact, I don't know if this has ever been done, but I'm going to give you the short version of this story—right here, right now—so you know what you're getting into. It goes like this:

I went to summer camp. I did some stuff. Some of it, I'm proud of. Some of it...not so much.

Then, before the full eight weeks of camp was up, things went kind of crazy (okay, a *lot* crazy), and I ended up packing my bags early.

It might have had something to do with this:

Or maybe it looked more like this:

It also could have had something to do with this:

Or with this:

And I can tell you for sure that it definitely had something to do with this:

Somewhere in all of that, there's an ending to this crazy story. There's some middle in there too. And yeah, okay, some of it didn't exactly happen like that. What can I say? I like to keep things interesting.

But don't worry. I'll always steer you straight...eventually.

The point is, my summer at Camp Wannamorra basically went the same way a lot of my life goes. There were some ups, some downs, some good luck, and a whole lot of bad luck before it all came crashing down around me in a giant ball of flame. (Not a real one—that was my last book.)

But that's as much as I'm going to tell you for now. If you want all the gory details, you're just going to have to read this whole thing.

Because, as the Booger-Eater always said, getting there is half the fun.

CHAPTER 2

WELCOME TO CAMP WANNAMORRA

You know those regular camps, where kids spend the summer running around in the fresh air, and roasting marshmallows, and swimming in the lake all day? Maybe you've even been to one of those places.

Well, hold that thought. Here's another question:

Have you ever read the book *Holes*? If you haven't, you should, because it's an awesome book. But there was a camp in that story too—Camp Green Lake, which was actually a prison for kids.

Let's say that the place I went, Camp Wannamorra, was somewhere right in the middle of all that. Half camp and half prison. And by *prison*, I mean school.

That's right. Me. Summer school. Again.

If you read my last two books, then you know that *school* isn't exactly my best subject. In fact,

I've already done time at Hills Village Middle School, Cathedral School of the Arts, *and* Airbrook Arts. (I'm kind of, sort of, an artist, but more about that later.) Crazy, right? Let's just say I move around a lot.

The bottom line: If I wanted to keep going to Airbrook, I was going to have to "do some work" over the summer. And we all know what that means.

So when Mom told me and my sister, Georgia, that she'd found the "perfect" camp for us, I was suspicious right away.

Every morning from eight to twelve at Camp Wannamorra, we would be in classes. I was going to take the kind for kids who needed a little extra help. And brainiac Georgia, who couldn't even wait to start middle school in the fall, was going to take the "Challenge Program," for kids who had nothing better to do during school vacation than get smarter than they already were.

The more Mom talked about it, the more excited Georgia became, which made me even more suspicious. She kept calling it "summer camp," but I was pretty sure it was going to look something like this:

Ready, set, and let's begin! The square root of one hundred is always ten!
Can someone turn the TV off? I'm trying to solve for x!
PHYSICS
ALGEBRA
MATH

Extra homework, please!
ALGEBRA 4 MILES
MOOZART
What are your thoughts on the protagonist's journey?
BEET
Too unrealisssstic.

Well, guess what? It turned out I was half-right about Camp Wannamorra. Some of it was exactly as terrible as I'd expected it to be.

Some of it was even *worse*.

READ MORE iN
MIDDLE SCHOOL:

HOW I SURVIVED
BULLIES,
BROCCOLI
~ AND ~
SNAKE HILL

DON'T CROSS THE DICTATOR

TEAM DEAD MEAT

The Serial Killer in the Next Bunk

Angry, but Imaginary

AN ILLUSTRATED NOVEL

Middle School
The Worst Years of My Life

James Patterson
& Chris Tebbetts

Illustrated by Laura Park

Rafe Khatchadorian has enough problems at home without throwing his first year of middle school into the mix. Luckily, he's got an ace plan for the best year ever, if only he can pull it off. With his best friend Leonardo the Silent awarding him points, Rafe tries to break every rule in his school's Code of Conduct. Chewing gum in class – 5,000 points! Running in the hallway – 10,000 points! Pulling the fire alarm – 50,000 points! But when Rafe's game starts to catch up with him, he'll have to decide if winning is all that matters, or if he's finally ready to face the rules, bullies, and truths he's been avoiding.

Containing over 100 brilliant illustrations, *Middle School* is the hilarious story of Rafe's attempt to somehow survive the very worst year of his life!

Middle School
Get Me Out of Here!

James Patterson
& Chris Tebbetts

Illustrated by Laura Park

After sixth grade, the very *worst* year of his life, Rafe Khatchadorian
thinks he has it made in seventh grade. He's been accepted to art
school in the big city and imagines a math-and-history-free fun
zone. *Wrong!* It's more competitive than Rafe ever expected, and
to score big in class, he needs to find a way to turn his boring life
into the inspiration for a work of art. His method? Operation: Get
a Life! Anything he's never done before, he's going to do it, from
learning to play poker to going to a modern art museum. But
when his newest mission uncovers secrets about the family
Rafe's never known, he has to decide if he's ready to have his
world turned upside down.

James Patterson's winning follow-up to *Middle School: The
Worst Years of My Life* is another riotous and heart-warming story
about living large.

A NEW ILLUSTRATED SERIES!

I Funny

James Patterson
& Chris Grabenstein

Illustrated by Laura Park

**Introducing James Patterson's most hilarious
character *ever*!**

Jamie Grimm is a middle schooler on a mission: he wants to
become the world's greatest stand-up comedian – even if he
always seems to 'choke' in the spotlight.

When Jamie finds out about a contest called the Funniest Kid on
the Planet, he knows it's time to face his fears and enter. But are
the judges rewarding him out of pity because he happens to be in
a wheelchair, like his bullying cousin Stevie suggests? And will
Jamie ever share the secret of his troubled past – and reason for
his disability – instead of hiding behind his comedy act?

In this highly illustrated book that's as heartfelt as it is hilarious,
James Patterson dishes out heaps of jokes that will have readers
rolling on the floor and cheering for more.

OUT NOW!

I Even Funnier

James Patterson
& Chris Grabenstein

Illustrated by Laura Park

The side-splittingly brilliant follow-up to *I Funny*

Middle schooler Jamie Grimm has big dreams of being the best stand-up comic in the world – and he won't let the fact that he's in a wheelchair get in his way.

After winning the New York state finals in the Planet's Funniest Kid Comic Contest, Jamie's off to Boston to compete in the national semi-finals. But when one of his best buddies runs into trouble at school and a sudden family health scare rears its head, Jamie has to put his comedic ambitions on hold and stand by the people he cares about.

Can Jamie pass up the big competition for the sake of his friends and family?

OUT NOW!

Treasure Hunters

James Patterson
& Chris Grabenstein

Illustrated by Juliana Neufeld

A new adventure series jam-packed with action, humour and heart!

The Kidd siblings have grown up travelling the world and diving down to shipwrecks, helping their famous parents recover everything from swords to gold doubloons from the bottom of the ocean. But after their parents disappear on the job, the kids are suddenly thrust into the biggest treasure hunt of their lives.

They'll have to work together to defeat dangerous pirates and dodge the hot pursuit of an evil treasure-hunting rival, all while following cryptic clues to unravel the mystery of what really happened to their parents – and find out if they're still alive.